Selected Stories by
G. K. CHESTERTON

Books in this Series:

Selected Stories by O. Henry
Selected Stories by Anton Chekhov
Selected Stories by Guy de Maupassant
Selected Stories by Mark Twain
Selected Stories by Edgar Allan Poe
Selected Stories by Rudyard Kipling
Selected Stories by Saki
Selected Stories by Oscar Wilde
Selected Stories by Honoré de Balzac
Selected Stories by Charles Dickens
Selected Stories by D.H. Lawrence
Selected Stories by H.G. Wells
Selected Stories by Jack London
Selected Stories by Joseph Conrad
Selected Stories by Leo Tolstoy
Selected Stories by Sir Arthur Conan Doyle
Selected Stories by James Joyce
Selected Stories by Virginia Woolf
Selected Stories by Thomas Hardy
Selected Stories by Fyodor Dostoyevsky
Selected Stories by Katherine Mansfield
Selected Stories by Wilkie Collins
Selected Stories by Robert Louis Stevenson
Selected Stories by Howard Pyle
Selected Stories by Jerome K. Jerome
Selected Stories by Sir Walter Scott
Selected Stories by H. Rider Haggard

Selected Stories by
G. K. CHESTERTON

Published by
Rupa Publications India Pvt. Ltd 2015
7/16, Ansari Road, Daryaganj
New Delhi 110002

Sales Centres:
Allahabad Bengaluru Chennai
Hyderabad Jaipur Kathmandu
Kolkata Mumbai

Selection and Introduction copyright © Terry O'Brien 2015

All rights reserved.
No part of this publication may be reproduced, transmitted,
or stored in a retrieval system, in any form or by any means,
electronic, mechanical, photocopying, recording or otherwise,
without the prior permission of the publisher.

ISBN: 978-81-291-3689-3

First impression 2015

10 9 8 7 6 5 4 3 2 1

Printed at Shree Maitery Printech Pvt. Ltd., Noida

This book is sold subject to the condition that it shall not,
by way of trade or otherwise, be lent, resold, hired out, or otherwise
circulated, without the publisher's prior consent, in any form of binding or
cover other than that in which it is published.

CONTENTS

Introduction		vii
1	The Absence of Mr Glass	1
2	The Awful Reason of the Vicar's Visit	18
3	The Blue Cross	38
4	The Bottomless Well	61
5	The Duel of Dr Hirsch	80
6	The Secret Garden	98

INTRODUCTION

Gilbert Keith Chesterton (29 May 1874–14 June 1936), better known as G. K. Chesterton, was an English writer, thinker, lay theologian, dramatist, and journalist. One of the most prolific writers of the twentieth century, over his lifetime Chesterton wrote a hundred books, hundreds of poems, five plays, five novels, about two hundred short stories, over 4000 newspaper essays, and thirteen years of weekly columns for *The Daily News* while also editing his own newspaper, *G.K.'s Weekly*.

Smart and incisive, Chesterton's style is unmistakable, always marked by humility, consistency and wit. He is often referred to as the 'prince of paradox' and was equally at ease across topics as varied as history, politics, economics, and philosophy.

This selection contains a few of his best stories, many of them featuring the popular priest-detective Father Brown:

- 'The Absence of Mr Glass' is from the collection *The Wisdom of Father Brown*. Doctor Orion Hood, a great psychological and criminological expert, is suddenly interrupted by a dishevelled man, stumbling over heavy load of luggage and an umbrella. It is Father Brown, the priest, come to ask his advice about two young lovers.
- In 'The Awful Reason of The Vicar's Visit', from the collection *The Club of Queer Trades*, Mr Swinburne, getting ready to go for a dinner party with Basil Grant, has a strange visitor. A distraught Vicar of Chuntsey calls on him to investigate a mysterious assault.

- 'The Blue Cross' is Chesterton's first story starring Father Brown. Aristide Valentin, head of Paris Police, is on the trail of the world-famous criminal Flambeau.
- 'The Bottomless Well' is from the collection *The Man Who Knew Too Much* and stars Horne Fisher, who investigates a variety of crimes that occur on aristocratic estates in pre-World War I Britain.
- 'The Duel of Dr Hirsch' is another gem from the collection *The Wisdom of Father Brown*. It concerns a crooked duel, with espionage involved.
- In 'The Secret Garden' Father Brown investigates a mystery which plays out in the home of renowned detective Aristide Valentin.

1

THE ABSENCE OF MR GLASS

The consulting-rooms of Dr Orion Hood, the eminent criminologist and specialist in certain moral disorders, lay along the sea-front at Scarborough, in a series of very large and well-lighted french windows, which showed the North Sea like one endless outer wall of blue-green marble. In such a place the sea had something of the monotony of a blue-green dado: for the chambers themselves were ruled throughout by a terrible tidiness not unlike the terrible tidiness of the sea. It must not be supposed that Dr Hood's apartments excluded luxury, or even poetry. These things were there, in their place; but one felt that they were never allowed out of their place. Luxury was there: there stood upon a special table eight or ten boxes of the best cigars; but they were built upon a plan so that the strongest were always nearest the wall and the mildest nearest the window. A tantalus containing three kinds of spirit, all of a liqueur excellence, stood always on this table of luxury; but the fanciful have asserted that the whisky, brandy, and rum seemed always to stand at the same level. Poetry was there: the left-hand corner of the room was lined with as complete a set of English classics as the right hand could show of English and foreign physiologists. But if one took a volume of Chaucer or Shelley from that rank, its absence irritated the mind like a gap in a man's front teeth. One could not say the books were never read; probably they were, but there was a sense of their being chained to their places, like the Bibles in the old churches. Dr

Hood treated his private book-shelf as if it were a public library. And if this strict scientific intangibility steeped even the shelves laden with lyrics and ballads and the tables laden with drink and tobacco, it goes without saying that yet more of such heathen holiness protected the other shelves that held the specialist's library, and the other tables that sustained the frail and even fairylike instruments of chemistry or mechanics.

Dr Hood paced the length of his string of apartments, bounded—as the boys' geographies say—on the east by the North Sea and on the west by the serried ranks of his sociological and criminologist library. He was clad in an artist's velvet, but with none of an artist's negligence; his hair was heavily shot with grey, but growing thick and healthy; his face was lean, but sanguine and expectant. Everything about him and his room indicated something at once rigid and restless, like that great northern sea by which (on pure principles of hygiene) he had built his home.

Fate, being in a funny mood, pushed the door open and introduced into those long, strict, sea-flanked apartments one who was perhaps the most startling opposite of them and their master. In answer to a curt but civil summons, the door opened inwards and there shambled into the room a shapeless little figure, which seemed to find its own hat and umbrella as unmanageable as a mass of luggage. The umbrella was a black and prosaic bundle long past repair; the hat was a broad-curved black hat, clerical but not common in England; the man was the very embodiment of all that is homely and helpless.

The doctor regarded the new-comer with a restrained astonishment, not unlike that he would have shown if some huge but obviously harmless sea-beast had crawled into his room. The new-comer regarded the doctor with that beaming but breathless geniality which characterizes a corpulent charwoman who has just managed to stuff herself into an omnibus. It is a rich confusion of social self-congratulation and bodily disarray. His hat tumbled to the carpet, his heavy umbrella slipped between his knees with a thud; he reached after the one and ducked after the other, but with an unimpaired smile on his round face spoke simultaneously as follows:

'My name is Brown. Pray excuse me. I've come about that business of the MacNabs. I have heard, you often help people out of such troubles. Pray excuse me if I am wrong.'

By this time he had sprawlingly recovered the hat, and made an odd little bobbing bow over it, as if setting everything quite right.

'I hardly understand you,' replied the scientist, with a cold intensity of manner. 'I fear you have mistaken the chambers. I am Dr Hood, and my work is almost entirely literary and educational. It is true that I have sometimes been consulted by the police in cases of peculiar difficulty and importance, but—'

'Oh, this is of the greatest importance,' broke in the little man called Brown. 'Why, her mother won't let them get engaged.' And he leaned back in his chair in radiant rationality.

The brows of Dr Hood were drawn down darkly, but the eyes under them were bright with something that might be anger or might be amusement. 'And still,' he said, 'I do not quite understand.'

'You see, they want to get married,' said the man with the clerical hat. 'Maggie MacNab and young Todhunter want to get married. Now, what can be more important than that?'

The great Orion Hood's scientific triumphs had deprived him of many things—some said of his health, others of his God; but they had not wholly despoiled him of his sense of the absurd. At the last plea of the ingenuous priest a chuckle broke out of him from inside, and he threw himself into an armchair in an ironical attitude of the consulting physician.

'Mr Brown,' he said gravely, 'it is quite fourteen and a half years since I was personally asked to test a personal problem: then it was the case of an attempt to poison the French President at a Lord Mayor's Banquet. It is now, I understand, a question of whether some friend of yours called Maggie is a suitable fiancee for some friend of hers called Todhunter. Well, Mr Brown, I am a sportsman. I will take it on. I will give the MacNab family my best advice, as good as I gave the French Republic and the King of England—no, better: fourteen years better. I have nothing else to do this afternoon. Tell me your story.'

The little clergyman called Brown thanked him with unquestionable warmth, but still with a queer kind of simplicity. It was rather as if he were thanking a stranger in a smoking-room for some trouble in passing the matches, than as if he were (as he was) practically thanking the Curator of Kew Gardens for coming with him into a field to find a four-leaved clover. With scarcely a semi-colon after his hearty thanks, the little man began his recital:

'I told you my name was Brown; well, that's the fact, and I'm the priest of the little Catholic Church I dare say you've seen beyond those straggly streets, where the town ends towards the north. In the last and straggliest of those streets which runs along the sea like a sea-wall there is a very honest but rather sharp-tempered member of my flock, a widow called MacNab. She has one daughter, and she lets lodgings, and between her and the daughter, and between her and the lodgers—well, I dare say there is a great deal to be said on both sides. At present she has only one lodger, the young man called Todhunter; but he has given more trouble than all the rest, for he wants to marry the young woman of the house.'

'And the young woman of the house,' asked Dr Hood, with huge and silent amusement, 'what does she want?'

'Why, she wants to marry him,' cried Father Brown, sitting

up eagerly. 'That is just the awful complication.'

'It is indeed a hideous enigma,' said Dr Hood.

'This young James Todhunter,' continued the cleric, 'is a very decent man so far as I know; but then nobody knows very much. He is a bright, brownish little fellow, agile like a monkey, clean-shaven like an actor, and obliging like a born courtier. He seems to have quite a pocketful of money, but nobody knows what his trade is. Mrs MacNab, therefore (being of a pessimistic turn), is quite sure it is something dreadful, and probably connected with dynamite. The dynamite must be of a shy and noiseless sort, for the poor fellow only shuts himself up for several hours of the day and studies something behind a locked door. He declares his privacy is temporary and justified, and promises to explain before the wedding. That is all that anyone knows for certain, but Mrs MacNab will tell you a great deal more than even she is certain of. You know how the tales grow like grass on such a patch of ignorance as that. There are tales of two voices heard talking in the room; though, when the door is opened, Todhunter is always found alone. There are tales of a mysterious tall man in a silk hat, who once came out of the sea-mists and apparently out of the sea, stepping softly across the sandy fields and through the small back garden at twilight, till he was heard talking to the lodger at his open window. The colloquy seemed to end in a quarrel. Todhunter dashed down his window with violence, and the man in the high hat melted into the sea-fog again. This story is told by the family with the fiercest mystification; but I really think Mrs MacNab prefers her own original tale: that the Other Man (or whatever it is) crawls out every night from the big box in the corner, which is kept locked all day. You see, therefore, how this sealed door of Todhunter's is treated as the gate of all the fancies and monstrosities of the "Thousand and One Nights". And yet there is the little fellow in his respectable black jacket, as punctual and innocent as a parlour clock. He pays his rent to the tick; he is practically a teetotaller; he is tirelessly kind with the younger children, and can keep them amused for a day on end; and, last and most urgent of all, he has made himself equally popular with the eldest daughter, who is ready to go to church with him tomorrow.'

A man warmly concerned with any large theories has always a relish for applying them to any triviality. The great specialist having condescended to the priest's simplicity, condescended expansively. He settled himself with comfort in his arm-chair and began to talk in the tone of a somewhat absent-minded lecturer:

'Even in a minute instance, it is best to look first to the main tendencies of Nature. A particular flower may not be dead in early winter, but the flowers are dying; a particular pebble may never be wetted with the tide, but the tide is coming in. To the scientific eye all human history is a series of collective movements, destructions or migrations, like the massacre of flies in winter or the return of birds in spring. Now the root fact in all history is Race. Race produces religion; Race produces legal and ethical wars. There is no stronger case than that of the wild, unworldly and perishing stock which we commonly call the Celts, of whom your friends the MacNabs are specimens. Small, swarthy, and of this dreamy and drifting blood, they accept easily the superstitious explanation of any incidents, just as they still accept (you will excuse me for saying) that superstitious explanation of all incidents which you and your Church represent. It is not remarkable that such people, with the sea moaning behind them and the Church (excuse me again) droning in front of them, should put fantastic features into what are probably plain events. You, with your small parochial responsibilities, see only this particular Mrs MacNab, terrified with this particular tale of two voices and a tall man out of the sea. But the man with the scientific imagination sees, as it were, the whole clans of MacNab scattered over the whole world, in its ultimate average as uniform as a tribe of birds. He sees thousands of Mrs MacNabs, in thousands of houses, dropping their little drop of morbidity in the tea-cups of their friends; he sees—'

Before the scientist could conclude his sentence, another and more impatient summons sounded from without; someone with swishing skirts was marshalled hurriedly down the corridor, and the door opened on a young girl, decently dressed but disordered and red-hot with haste. She had sea-blown blonde hair, and would have been entirely beautiful if her cheek-bones had not been, in the Scotch manner, a little high in relief as well as in colour. Her apology was almost as abrupt as a command.

'I'm sorry to interrupt you, sir,' she said, 'but I had to follow Father Brown at once; it's nothing less than life or death.'

Father Brown began to get to his feet in some disorder. 'Why, what has happened, Maggie?' he said.

'James has been murdered, for all I can make out,' answered the girl, still breathing hard from her rush. 'That man Glass has been with him again; I heard them talking through the door quite plain. Two separate voices: for James speaks low, with a burr, and the other voice was high and quavery.'

'That man Glass?' repeated the priest in some perplexity.

'I know his name is Glass,' answered the girl, in great impatience. 'I heard it through the door. They were quarrelling—about money, I think—for I heard James say again and again, "That's right, Mr Glass," or "No, Mr Glass," and then, "Two or three, Mr Glass." But we're talking too much; you must come at once, and there may be time yet.'

'But time for what?' asked Dr Hood, who had been studying the young lady with marked interest. 'What is there about Mr Glass and his money troubles that should impel such urgency?'

'I tried to break down the door and couldn't,' answered the

girl shortly, 'Then I ran to the back-yard, and managed to climb on to the window-sill that looks into the room. It was all dim, and seemed to be empty, but I swear I saw James lying huddled up in a corner, as if he were drugged or strangled.'

'This is very serious,' said Father Brown, gathering his errant hat and umbrella and standing up; 'in point of fact I was just putting your case before this gentleman, and his view—'

'Has been largely altered,' said the scientist gravely. 'I do not think this young lady is so Celtic as I had supposed. As I have nothing else to do, I will put on my hat and stroll down town with you.'

In a few minutes all three were approaching the dreary tail of the MacNabs' street: the girl with the stern and breathless stride of the mountaineer, the criminologist with a lounging grace (which was not without a certain leopard-like swiftness), and the priest at an energetic trot entirely devoid of distinction. The aspect of this edge of the town was not entirely without justification for the doctor's hints about desolate moods and environments. The scattered houses stood farther and farther apart in a broken string along the seashore; the afternoon was closing with a premature and partly lurid twilight; the sea was of an inky purple and murmuring ominously. In the scrappy back garden of the MacNabs which ran down towards the sand, two black, barren-looking trees stood up like demon hands held up in astonishment, and as Mrs MacNab ran down the street to meet them with lean hands similarly spread, and her fierce face in shadow, she was a little like a demon herself. The doctor and the priest made scant reply to her shrill reiterations of her daughter's story, with more disturbing details of her own, to the divided vows of vengeance against Mr Glass for murdering, and against Mr Todhunter for being murdered, or against the latter for having dared to want to marry her daughter, and for not having lived to do it. They passed through the narrow passage in the front of the house until they came to the lodger's door at the back, and there Dr Hood, with the trick of an old detective, put his shoulder sharply to the panel and burst in the door.

It opened on a scene of silent catastrophe. No one seeing it, even for a flash, could doubt that the room had been the theatre of some thrilling collision between two, or perhaps more, persons. Playing-cards lay littered across the table or fluttered about the floor as if a game had been interrupted. Two wine glasses stood ready for wine on a side-table, but a third lay smashed in a star of crystal upon the carpet. A few feet from it lay what looked like a long knife or short sword, straight, but with an ornamental and pictured handle, its dull blade just caught a grey glint from the dreary window behind, which showed the black trees against the leaden level of the sea. Towards the opposite corner of the room was rolled a gentleman's silk top hat, as if it had just been knocked off his head; so much so, indeed, that one almost looked to see it still rolling. And in the corner behind it, thrown like a sack of potatoes, but corded like a railway trunk, lay Mr James Todhunter, with a scarf across his mouth, and six or seven ropes knotted round his elbows and ankles. His brown eyes were alive and shifted alertly.

Dr Orion Hood paused for one instant on the doormat and drank in the whole scene of voiceless violence. Then he stepped swiftly across the carpet, picked up the tall silk hat, and gravely put it upon the head of the yet pinioned Todhunter. It was so much too large for him that it almost slipped down on to his shoulders.

'Mr Glass's hat,' said the doctor, returning with it and peering into the inside with a pocket lens. 'How to explain the absence of Mr Glass and the presence of Mr Glass's hat? For Mr Glass is not a careless man with his clothes. That hat is of a stylish shape and systematically brushed and burnished, though not very new. An old dandy, I should think.'

'But, good heavens!' called out Miss MacNab, 'aren't you going to untie the man first?'

'I say "old" with intention, though not with certainty' continued the expositor; 'my reason for it might seem a little far-fetched. The hair of human beings falls out in very varying degrees, but almost always falls out slightly, and with the lens I should see the tiny hairs in a hat recently worn. It has none, which leads me to guess that Mr Glass is bald. Now when this is taken with the high-pitched and querulous voice which Miss MacNab described so vividly (patience, my dear lady, patience), when we take the hairless head together with the tone common in senile anger, I should think we may deduce some advance in years. Nevertheless, he was probably vigorous, and he was almost certainly tall. I might rely in some degree on the story of his previous appearance at the window, as a tall man in a silk hat, but I think I have more exact indication. This wineglass has been smashed all over the place, but one of its splinters lies on the high bracket beside the mantelpiece. No such fragment could have fallen there if the vessel had been smashed in the hand of a comparatively short man like Mr Todhunter.'

'By the way,' said Father Brown, 'might it not be as well to untie Mr Todhunter?'

'Our lesson from the drinking-vessels does not end here,' proceeded the specialist. 'I may say at once that it is possible that the man Glass was bald or nervous through dissipation rather than age. Mr Todhunter, as has been remarked, is a quiet thrifty gentleman, essentially an abstainer. These cards and wine cups are no part of his normal habit; they have been produced for a particular companion. But, as it happens, we may go farther. Mr Todhunter may or may not possess this wine-service, but there is no appearance of his possessing any wine. What, then, were these vessels to contain? I would at once suggest some brandy or whisky, perhaps of a luxurious sort, from a flask in the pocket of Mr Glass. We have thus something like a picture of the man, or at least of the type: tall, elderly, fashionable, but somewhat frayed, certainly fond of play and strong waters, perhaps rather too fond of them. Mr Glass is a gentleman not unknown on the fringes of society.'

'Look here,' cried the young woman, 'if you don't let me pass to untie him I'll run outside and scream for the police.'

'I should not advise you, Miss MacNab,' said Dr Hood gravely, 'to be in any hurry to fetch the police. Father Brown, I seriously ask you to compose your flock, for their sakes, not for mine. Well, we have seen something of the figure and quality of Mr Glass; what are the chief facts known of Mr Todhunter? They are substantially three: that he is economical, that he is more or less wealthy, and that he has a secret. Now, surely it is obvious that there are the three chief marks of the kind of man who is blackmailed. And surely it is equally obvious that the faded finery, the profligate habits, and the shrill irritation of Mr Glass are the unmistakable marks of the kind of man who blackmails him. We have the two typical figures of a tragedy of hush money: on the one hand, the respectable man with a mystery; on the other, the West-end vulture with a scent for a mystery. These two men have met here today and have quarrelled, using blows and a bare weapon.'

'Are you going to take those ropes off?' asked the girl stubbornly.

Dr Hood replaced the silk hat carefully on the side table, and went across to the captive. He studied him intently, even moving him a little and half-turning him round by the shoulders, but he only answered:

'No; I think these ropes will do very well till your friends the police bring the handcuffs.'

Father Brown, who had been looking dully at the carpet,

lifted his round face and said: 'What do you mean?'

The man of science had picked up the peculiar dagger-sword from the carpet and was examining it intently as he answered:

'Because you find Mr Todhunter tied up,' he said, 'you all jump to the conclusion that Mr Glass had tied him up; and then, I suppose, escaped. There are four objections to this: First, why should a gentleman so dressy as our friend Glass leave his hat behind him, if he left of his own free will? Second,' he continued, moving towards the window, 'this is the only exit, and it is locked on the inside. Third, this blade here has a tiny touch of blood at the point, but there is no wound on Mr Todhunter. Mr Glass took that wound away with him, dead or alive. Add to all this primary probability. It is much more likely that the blackmailed person would try to kill his incubus, rather than that the blackmailer would try to kill the goose that lays his golden egg. There, I think, we have a pretty complete story.'

'But the ropes?' inquired the priest, whose eyes had remained open with a rather vacant admiration.

'Ah, the ropes,' said the expert with a singular intonation. 'Miss MacNab very much wanted to know why I did not set Mr Todhunter free from his ropes. Well, I will tell her. I did not do it because Mr Todhunter can set himself free from them at any minute he chooses.'

'What?' cried the audience on quite different notes of astonishment.

'I have looked at all the knots on Mr Todhunter,' reiterated Hood quietly. 'I happen to know something about knots; they are quite a branch of criminal science. Every one of those knots he has made himself and could loosen himself; not one of them would have been made by an enemy really trying to pinion him. The whole of this affair of the ropes is a clever fake, to make us think him the victim of the struggle instead of the wretched

Glass, whose corpse may be hidden in the garden or stuffed up the chimney.'

There was a rather depressed silence; the room was darkening, the sea-blighted boughs of the garden trees looked leaner and blacker than ever, yet they seemed to have come nearer to the window. One could almost fancy they were sea-monsters like krakens or cuttlefish, writhing polypi who had crawled up from the sea to see the end of this tragedy, even as he, the villain and victim of it, the terrible man in the tall hat, had once crawled up from the sea. For the whole air was dense with the morbidity of blackmail, which is the most morbid of human things, because it is a crime concealing a crime; a black plaster on a blacker wound.

The face of the little Catholic priest, which was commonly complacent and even comic, had suddenly become knotted with a curious frown. It was not the blank curiosity of his first innocence. It was rather that creative curiosity which comes when a man has the beginnings of an idea. 'Say it again, please,' he said in a simple, bothered manner; 'do you mean that Todhunter can tie himself up all alone and untie himself all alone?'

'That is what I mean,' said the doctor.

'Jerusalem!' ejaculated Brown suddenly, 'I wonder if it could possibly be that!'

He scuttled across the room rather like a rabbit, and peered with quite a new impulsiveness into the partially-covered face of the captive. Then he turned his own rather fatuous face to the company. 'Yes, that's it!' he cried in a certain excitement. 'Can't you see it in the man's face? Why, look at his eyes!'

Both the Professor and the girl followed the direction of his glance. And though the broad black scarf completely masked the lower half of Todhunter's visage, they did grow conscious of something struggling and intense about the upper part of it.

'His eyes do look queer,' cried the young woman, strongly moved. 'You brutes; I believe it's hurting him!'

'Not that, I think,' said Dr Hood; 'the eyes have certainly a singular expression. But I should interpret those transverse wrinkles as expressing rather such slight psychological abnormality—'

'Oh, bosh!' cried Father Brown: 'can't you see he's laughing?'

'Laughing!' repeated the doctor, with a start; 'but what on earth can he be laughing at?'

'Well,' replied the Reverend Brown apologetically, 'not to put too fine a point on it, I think he is laughing at you. And indeed, I'm a little inclined to laugh at myself, now I know about it.'

'Now you know about what?' asked Hood, in some exasperation.

'Now I know,' replied the priest, 'the profession of Mr Todhunter.'

He shuffled about the room, looking at one object after another with what seemed to be a vacant stare, and then invariably bursting into an equally vacant laugh, a highly irritating process for those who had to watch it. He laughed very much over the hat, still more uproariously over the broken glass, but the blood on the sword point sent him into mortal convulsions of amusement. Then he turned to the fuming specialist.

'Dr Hood,' he cried enthusiastically, 'you are a great poet! You have called an uncreated being out of the void. How much more godlike that is than if you had only ferreted out the mere facts! Indeed, the mere facts are rather commonplace and comic by comparison.'

'I have no notion what you are talking about,' said Dr Hood rather haughtily; 'my facts are all inevitable, though necessarily incomplete. A place may be permitted to intuition, perhaps (or poetry if you prefer the term), but only because the corresponding details cannot as yet be ascertained. In the absence of Mr Glass—'

'That's it, that's it,' said the little priest, nodding quite eagerly, 'that's the first idea to get fixed; the absence of Mr Glass. He is so extremely absent. I suppose,' he added reflectively, 'that there was never anybody so absent as Mr Glass.'

'Do you mean he is absent from the town?' demanded the doctor.

'I mean he is absent from everywhere,' answered Father Brown; 'he is absent from the Nature of Things, so to speak.'

'Do you seriously mean,' said the specialist with a smile, 'that there is no such person?'

The priest made a sign of assent. 'It does seem a pity,' he said.

Orion Hood broke into a contemptuous laugh. 'Well,' he said, 'before we go on to the hundred and one other evidences, let us take the first proof we found; the first fact we fell over when we fell into this room. If there is no Mr Glass, whose hat is this?'

'It is Mr Todhunter's,' replied Father Brown.

'But it doesn't fit him,' cried Hood impatiently. 'He couldn't possibly wear it!'

Father Brown shook his head with ineffable mildness. 'I never said he could wear it,' he answered. 'I said it was his hat. Or, if you insist on a shade of difference, a hat that is his.'

'And what is the shade of difference?' asked the criminologist with a slight sneer.

'My good sir,' cried the mild little man, with his first movement akin to impatience, 'if you will walk down the street to the nearest hatter's shop, you will see that there is, in common speech, a difference between a man's hat and the hats that are his.'

'But a hatter,' protested Hood, 'can get money out of his

stock of new hats. What could Todhunter get out of this one old hat?'

'Rabbits,' replied Father Brown promptly.

'What?' cried Dr Hood.

'Rabbits, ribbons, sweetmeats, goldfish, rolls of coloured paper,' said the reverend gentleman with rapidity. 'Didn't you see it all when you found out the faked ropes? It's just the same with the sword. Mr Todhunter hasn't got a scratch on him, as you say; but he's got a scratch in him, if you follow me.'

'Do you mean inside Mr Todhunter's clothes?' inquired Mrs MacNab sternly.

'I do not mean inside Mr Todhunter's clothes,' said Father Brown. 'I mean inside Mr Todhunter.'

'Well, what in the name of Bedlam do you mean?'

'Mr Todhunter,' explained Father Brown placidly, 'is learning to be a professional conjurer, as well as juggler, ventriloquist, and expert in the rope trick. The conjuring explains the hat. It is without traces of hair, not because it is worn by the prematurely bald Mr Glass, but because it has never been worn by anybody. The juggling explains the three glasses, which Todhunter was teaching himself to throw up and catch in rotation. But, being only at the stage of practice, he smashed one glass against the ceiling. And the juggling also explains the sword, which it was Mr Todhunter's professional pride and duty to swallow. But, again, being at the stage of practice, he very slightly grazed the inside of his throat with the weapon. Hence he has a wound inside him, which I am sure (from the expression on his face) is not a serious one. He was also practising the trick of a release from ropes, like the Davenport Brothers, and he was just about to free himself when we all burst into the room. The cards, of course, are for card tricks, and they are scattered on the floor because he had just been practising one of those dodges of sending them flying through the air. He merely kept his trade secret, because he had to keep his tricks secret, like any other conjurer. But the mere fact of an idler in a top hat having once looked in at his back window, and been driven away by him with great indignation, was enough to set us all on a wrong track of romance, and make us imagine his whole life overshadowed by the silk-hatted spectre of Mr Glass.'

'But what about the two voices?' asked Maggie, staring.

'Have you never heard a ventriloquist?' asked Father Brown. 'Don't you know they speak first in their natural voice, and then answer themselves in just that shrill, squeaky, unnatural voice that you heard?'

There was a long silence, and Dr Hood regarded the little man who had spoken with a dark and attentive smile. 'You are certainly a very ingenious person,' he said; 'it could not have been done better in a book. But there is just one part of Mr Glass you have not succeeded in explaining away, and that is his name. Miss MacNab distinctly heard him so addressed by Mr Todhunter.'

The Rev Mr Brown broke into a rather childish giggle. 'Well, that,' he said, 'that's the silliest part of the whole silly story. When our juggling friend here threw up the three glasses in turn, he counted them aloud as he caught them, and also commented aloud when he failed to catch them. What he really said was: "One, two and three—missed a glass one, two—missed a glass." And so on.'

There was a second of stillness in the room, and then everyone with one accord burst out laughing. As they did so the figure in the corner complacently uncoiled all the ropes and let them fall with a flourish. Then, advancing into the middle of the room with a bow, he produced from his pocket a big bill printed in blue and red, which announced that ZALADIN, the World's Greatest Conjurer, Contortionist, Ventriloquist and Human Kangaroo would be ready with an entirely new series of Tricks at the Empire Pavilion, Scarborough, on Monday next at eight o'clock precisely.

2

THE AWFUL REASON OF THE VICAR'S VISIT

The revolt of Matter against Man (which I believe to exist) has now been reduced to a singular condition. It is the small things rather than the large things which make war against us and, I may add, beat us. The bones of the last mammoth have long ago decayed, a mighty wreck; the tempests no longer devour our navies, nor the mountains with hearts of fire heap hell over our cities. But we are engaged in a bitter and eternal war with small things; chiefly with microbes and with collar studs. The stud with which I was engaged (on fierce and equal terms) as I made the above reflections, was one which I was trying to introduce into my shirt collar when a loud knock came at the door.

My first thought was as to whether Basil Grant had called to fetch me. He and I were to turn up at the same dinner-party (for which I was in the act of dressing), and it might be that he had taken it into his head to come my way, though we had arranged to go separately. It was a small and confidential affair at the table of a good but unconventional political lady, an old friend of his. She had asked us both to meet a third guest, a Captain Fraser, who had made something of a name and was an authority on chimpanzees. As Basil was an old friend of the hostess and I had never seen her, I felt that it was quite possible that he (with his usual social sagacity) might have decided to take me along in order to break the ice. The theory, like all my theories, was complete; but as a fact it was not Basil.

I was handed a visiting card inscribed: 'Rev. Ellis Shorter', and underneath was written in pencil, but in a hand in which even hurry could not conceal a depressing and gentlemanly excellence, 'Asking the favour of a few moments' conversation on a most urgent matter.'!

I had already subdued the stud, thereby proclaiming that the image of God has supremacy over all matters (a valuable truth), and throwing on my dress-coat and waistcoat, hurried into the drawing-room. He rose at my entrance, flapping like a seal; I can use no other description. He flapped a plaid shawl over his right arm; he flapped a pair of pathetic black gloves; he flapped his clothes; I may say, without exaggeration, that he flapped his eyelids, as he rose. He was a bald-browed, white-haired, white-whiskered old clergyman, of a flappy and floppy type. He said:

'I am so sorry. I am so very sorry. I am so extremely sorry. I come—I can only say—I can only say in my defence, that I come—upon an important matter. Pray forgive me.'

I told him I forgave perfectly and waited.

'What I have to say,' he said brokenly, 'is so dreadful—it is so dreadful—I have lived a quiet life.'

I was burning to get away, for it was already doubtful if I should be in time for dinner. But there was something about the old man's honest air of bitterness that seemed to open to me the possibilities of life larger and more tragic than my own.

I said gently: 'Pray go on.'

Nevertheless the old gentleman, being a gentleman as well as old, noticed my secret impatience and seemed still more unmanned.

'I'm so sorry,' he said meekly; 'I wouldn't have come—but for—your friend Major Brown recommended me to come here.'

'Major Brown!' I said, with some interest.

'Yes,' said the Reverend Mr Shorter, feverishly flapping his plaid shawl about. 'He told me you helped him in a great difficulty—and my difficulty! Oh, my dear sir, it's a matter of life and death.'

I rose abruptly, in an acute perplexity. 'Will it take long, Mr Shorter?' I asked. 'I have to go out to dinner almost at once.'

He rose also, trembling from head to foot, and yet somehow, with all his moral palsy, he rose to the dignity of his age and his office.

'I have no right, Mr Swinburne—I have no right at all,' he said. 'If you have to go out to dinner, you have of course—a perfect right—of course a perfect right. But when you come back—a man will be dead.'

And he sat down, quaking like a jelly.

The triviality of the dinner had been in those two minutes dwarfed and drowned in my mind. I did not want to go and see a political widow, and a captain who collected apes; I wanted to hear what had brought this dear, doddering old vicar into relation with immediate perils.

'Will you have a cigar?' I said.

'No, thank you,' he said, with indescribable embarrassment, as if not smoking cigars was a social disgrace.

'A glass of wine?' I said.

'No, thank you, no, thank you; not just now,' he repeated with that hysterical eagerness with which people who do not drink at all often try to convey that on any other night of the week they would sit up all night drinking rum-punch. 'Not just now, thank you.'

'Nothing else I can get for you?' I said, feeling genuinely sorry for the well-mannered old donkey. 'A cup of tea?'

I saw a struggle in his eye and I conquered. When the cup of tea came he drank it like a dipsomaniac gulping brandy. Then he fell back and said:

'I have had such a time, Mr Swinburne. I am not used to these excitements. As Vicar of Chuntsey, in Essex'—he threw this in with an indescribable airiness of vanity—'I have never known such things happen.'

'What things happen?' I asked.

He straightened himself with sudden dignity.

'As Vicar of Chuntsey, in Essex,' he said, 'I have never been forcibly dressed up as an old woman and made to take part in a crime in the character of an old woman. Never once. My experience may be small. It may be insufficient. But it has never occurred to me before.'

'I have never heard of it,' I said, 'as among the duties of a clergyman. But I am not well up in church matters. Excuse me if perhaps I failed to follow you correctly. Dressed up—as what?'

'As an old woman,' said the vicar solemnly, 'as an old woman.'

I thought in my heart that it required no great transformation to make an old woman of him, but the thing was evidently more tragic than comic, and I said respectfully:

'May I ask how it occurred?'

'I will begin at the beginning,' said Mr Shorter, 'and I will tell my story with the utmost possible precision. At seventeen minutes past eleven this morning I left the vicarage to keep certain appointments and pay certain visits in the village. My first visit was to Mr Jervis, the treasurer of our League of Christian Amusements, with whom I concluded some business touching the claim made by Parkes the gardener in the matter of the rolling of our tennis lawn. I then visited Mrs Arnett, a very earnest churchwoman, but permanently bedridden. She is the author of several small works of devotion, and of a book of verse, entitled (unless my memory misleads me) Eglantine.'

He uttered all this not only with deliberation, but with something that can only be called, by a contradictory phrase, eager deliberation. He had, I think, a vague memory in his head of the detectives in the detective stories, who always sternly require that nothing should be kept back.

'I then proceeded,' he went on, with the same maddening conscientiousness of manner, 'to Mr Carr (not Mr James Carr, of course; Mr Robert Carr) who is temporarily assisting our organist, and having consulted with him (on the subject of a choir boy who is accused, I cannot as yet say whether justly or not, of cutting holes in the organ pipes), I finally dropped in upon a Dorcas meeting at the house of Miss Brett. The Dorcas meetings are usually held at the vicarage, but my wife being unwell, Miss Brett, a newcomer in our village, but very active in church work, had very kindly consented to hold them. The Dorcas society is entirely under my wife's management as a rule, and except for Miss Brett, who, as I say, is very active, I scarcely know any members of it. I had, however, promised to drop in on them, and I did so.

'When I arrived there were only four other maiden ladies with Miss Brett, but they were sewing very busily. It is very difficult, of course, for any person, however strongly impressed with the necessity in these matters of full and exact exposition of the facts, to remember and repeat the actual details of a conversation, particularly a conversation which (though inspired with a most worthy and admirable zeal for good work) was one which did not greatly impress the hearer's mind at the time and was in fact—er—mostly about socks. I can, however, remember distinctly that one of the spinster ladies (she was a thin person with a woollen shawl, who appeared to feel the cold, and I am almost sure she was introduced to me as Miss James) remarked that the weather was very changeable. Miss Brett then offered me a cup of tea, which I accepted, I cannot recall in what words. Miss Brett is a short and stout lady with white hair. The only other figure in the group that caught my attention was a Miss Mowbray, a small and neat lady of aristocratic manners, silver hair, and a high voice and colour. She was the most emphatic member of the party; and her views on the subject of pinafores, though expressed with a natural deference to myself, were in themselves strong and advanced. Beside her (although all five ladies were dressed simply in black) it could not be denied that the others looked in some way what you men of the world would call dowdy.

'After about ten minutes' conversation I rose to go, and as I did so I heard something which—I cannot describe it—something which seemed to—but I really cannot describe it.'

'What did you hear?' I asked, with some impatience.

'I heard,' said the vicar solemnly, 'I heard Miss Mowbray (the lady with the silver hair) say to Miss James (the lady with the woollen shawl), the following extraordinary words. I committed them to memory on the spot, and as soon as circumstances set me free to do so, I noted them down on a piece of paper. I believe I have it here.' He fumbled in his breast-pocket, bringing out mild things, note-books, circulars and programmes of village concerts. 'I heard Miss Mowbray say to Miss James, the following words: "Now's your time, Bill."'

He gazed at me for a few moments after making this announcement, gravely and unflinchingly, as if conscious that here he was unshaken about his facts. Then he resumed, turning his bald head more towards the fire.

'This appeared to me remarkable. I could not by any means understand it. It seemed to me first of all peculiar that one maiden lady should address another maiden lady as "Bill". My experience, as I have said, may be incomplete; maiden ladies may have among themselves and in exclusively spinster circles wilder customs than I am aware of. But it seemed to me odd, and I could almost have sworn (if you will not misunderstand the phrase), I should have been strongly impelled to maintain at the time that the words, "Now's your time, Bill", were by no means pronounced with that upper-class intonation which, as I have already said, had up to now characterized Miss Mowbray's conversation. In fact, the words, "Now's your time, Bill", would have been, I fancy, unsuitable if pronounced with that upper-class intonation.

'I was surprised, I repeat, then, at the remark. But I was still more surprised when, looking round me in bewilderment, my hat and umbrella in hand, I saw the lean lady with the woollen shawl leaning upright against the door out of which I was just about to make my exit. She was still knitting, and I supposed that this erect posture against the door was only an eccentricity of spinsterhood and an oblivion of my intended departure.

'I said genially, "I am so sorry to disturb you, Miss James, but I must really be going. I have—er—" I stopped here, for the words she had uttered in reply, though singularly brief and in tone extremely business-like, were such as to render that arrest of my remarks, I think, natural and excusable. I have these words also noted down. I have not the least idea of their meaning; so I have only been able to render them phonetically. But she said,' and Mr Shorter peered short-sightedly at his papers, 'she said: "Chuck it, fat 'ead," and she added something that sounded like "It's a kop", or (possibly) "a kopt". And then the last cord, either of my sanity or the sanity of the universe, snapped suddenly. My esteemed friend and helper, Miss Brett, standing by the mantelpiece, said: "Put 'is old 'ead in a bag, Sam, and tie 'im up before you start jawin'. You'll be kopt yourselves some o' these days with this way of coin' things, har lar theater."

'My head went round and round. Was it really true, as I had suddenly fancied a moment before, that unmarried ladies had some dreadful riotous society of their own from which all others were excluded? I remembered dimly in my classical days (I was a scholar in a small way once, but now, alas! rusty), I remembered the mysteries of the Bona Dea and their strange female freemasonry. I remembered the witches' Sabbaths. I was just, in my absurd light-headedness, trying to remember a line of verse about Diana's nymphs, when Miss Mowbray threw her arm round me from behind. The moment it held me I knew it was not a woman's arm.

'Miss Brett—or what I had called Miss Brett—was standing in front of me with a big revolver in her hand and a broad grin on her face. Miss James was still leaning against the door, but had fallen into an attitude so totally new, and so totally unfeminine, that it gave one a shock. She was kicking her heels, with her hands in her pockets and her cap on one side. She was a man. I mean he was a wo—no, that is I saw that instead of being a woman she—he, I mean—that is, it was a man.'

Mr Shorter became indescribably flurried and flapping in endeavouring to arrange these genders and his plaid shawl at the same time. He resumed with a higher fever of nervousness:

'As for Miss Mowbray, she—he, held me in a ring of iron. He had her arm—that is she had his arm—round her neck—my neck I mean—and I could not cry out. Miss Brett—that is, Mr Brett, at least Mr something who was not Miss Brett—had the revolver pointed at me. The other two ladies—or er—gentlemen, were rummaging in some bag in the background. It was all clear at last: they were criminals dressed up as women, to kidnap me! To kidnap the Vicar of Chuntsey, in Essex. But why? Was it to be Nonconformists?

'The brute leaning against the door called out carelessly, '"Urry up, 'Arry. Show the old bloke what the game is, and let's get off."

'"Curse 'is eyes," said Miss Brett—I mean the man with the revolver—"why should we show 'im the game?"

'"If you take my advice you bloomin' well will," said the man at the door, whom they called Bill. "A man wot knows wet 'e's doin' is worth ten wot don't, even if 'e's a potty old parson."

"'Bill's right enough," said the coarse voice of the man who held me (it had been Miss Mowbray's). "Bring out the picture, 'Arry."

'The man with the revolver walked across the room to where the other two women—I mean men—were turning over baggage, and asked them for something which they gave him. He came back with it across the room and held it out in front of me. And compared to the surprise of that display, all the previous surprises of this awful day shrank suddenly.

'It was a portrait of myself. That such a picture should be in the hands of these scoundrels might in any case have caused a mild surprise; but no more. It was no mild surprise that I felt. The likeness was an extremely good one, worked up with all the accessories of the conventional photographic studio. I was leaning my head on my hand and was relieved against a painted landscape of woodland. It was obvious that it was no snapshot; it was clear that I had sat for this photograph. And the truth was that I had never sat for such a photograph. It was a photograph that I had never had taken.

'I stared at it again and again. It seemed to me to be touched up a good deal; it was glazed as well as framed, and the glass blurred some of the details. But there unmistakably was my face, my eyes, my nose and mouth, my head and hand, posed for a professional photographer. And I had never posed so for any photographer.

'"Be'old the bloomin' miracle," said the man with the revolver, with ill-timed facetiousness. "Parson, prepare to meet your God." And with this he slid the glass out of the frame. As the glass moved, I saw that part of the picture was painted on it in Chinese white, notably a pair of white whiskers and a clerical collar. And underneath was a portrait of an old lady in a quiet black dress, leaning her head on her hand against the woodland landscape. The old lady was as like me as one pin is like another. It had required only the whiskers and the collar to make it me in every hair.

"'Entertainin', ain't it?" said the man described as 'Arry, as he shot the glass back again. "Remarkable resemblance, parson. Gratifyin' to the lady. Gratifyin' to you. And hi may hadd, particlery gratifyin' to us, as bein' the probable source of a very tolerable haul. You know Colonel Hawker, the man who's come to live in these parts, don't you?"

'I nodded.

"'Well," said the man 'Arry, pointing to the picture, "that's 'is mother. 'Oo ran to catch 'im when 'e fell? She did," and he flung his fingers in a general gesture towards the photograph of the old lady who was exactly like me.

"'Tell the old gent wot 'e's got to do and be done with it," broke out Bill from the door. "Look 'ere, Reverend Shorter, we ain't goin' to do you no 'arm. We'll give you a sov. for your trouble if you like. And as for the old woman's clothes—why, you'll look lovely in 'em."

"'You ain't much of a 'and at a description, Bill," said the man behind me. "Mr Shorter, it's like this. We've got to see this man Hawker tonight. Maybe 'e'll kiss us all and 'ave up the champagne when 'e sees us. Maybe on the other 'and—'e won't. Maybe 'e'll be dead when we goes away. Maybe not. But we've got to see 'im. Now as you know, 'e shuts 'isself up and never opens the door to a soul; only you don't know why and we does. The only one as can ever get at 'im is 'is mother. Well, it's a confounded funny coincidence," he said, accenting the penultimate, "it's a very unusual piece of good luck, but you're 'is mother."

"'When first I saw 'er picture," said the man Bill, shaking his head in a ruminant manner, "when I first saw it I said—old Shorter. Those were my exact words—old Shorter."

"'What do you mean, you wild creatures?" I gasped. "What am I to do?"

'"That's easy said, your 'oldness," said the man with the revolver, good-humouredly; "you've got to put on those clothes," and he pointed to a poke-bonnet and a heap of female clothes in the corner of the room.

'I will not dwell, Mr Swinburne, upon the details of what followed. I had no choice. I could not fight five men, to say nothing of a loaded pistol. In five minutes, sir, the Vicar of Chuntsey was dressed as an old woman—as somebody else's mother, if you please—and was dragged out of the house to take part in a crime.

'It was already late in the afternoon, and the nights of winter were closing in fast. On a dark road, in a blowing wind, we set out towards the lonely house of Colonel Hawker, perhaps the queerest cortege that ever straggled up that or any other road. To every human eye, in every external, we were six very respectable old ladies of small means, in black dresses and refined but antiquated bonnets; and we were really five criminals and a clergyman.

'I will cut a long story short. My brain was whirling like a windmill as I walked, trying to think of some manner of escape. To cry out, so long as we were far from houses, would be suicidal, for it would be easy for the ruffians to knife me or to gag me and fling me into a ditch. On the other hand, to attempt to stop strangers and explain the situation was impossible, because of the frantic folly of the situation itself. Long before I had persuaded the chance postman or carrier of so absurd a story, my companions would certainly have got off themselves, and in all probability would have carried me off, as a friend of theirs who had the misfortune to be mad or drunk. The last thought, however, was an inspiration; though a very terrible one. Had it come to this, that the Vicar of Chuntsey must pretend to be mad or drunk? It had come to this.

'I walked along with the rest up the deserted road, imitating and keeping pace, as far as I could, with their rapid and yet lady-like step, until at length I saw a lamp-post and a policeman standing under it. I had made up my mind. Until we reached them we were all equally demure and silent and swift. When we reached them I suddenly flung myself against the railings and roared out: "Hooray! Hooray! Hooray! Rule Britannia! Get your 'air cut. Hoop-la! Boo!" It was a condition of no little novelty for a man in my position.

'The constable instantly flashed his lantern on me, or the draggled, drunken old woman that was my travesty. "Now then, mum," he began gruffly.

'"Come along quiet, or I'll eat your heart," cried Sam in my ear hoarsely. "Stop, or I'll flay you." It was frightful to hear the words and see the neatly shawled old spinster who whispered them.

'I yelled, and yelled—I was in for it now. I screamed comic refrains that vulgar young men had sung, to my regret, at our village concerts; I rolled to and fro like a ninepin about to fall.

'"If you can't get your friend on quiet, ladies," said the policeman, "I shall have to take 'er up. Drunk and disorderly she is right enough."

'I redoubled my efforts. I had not been brought up to this sort of thing; but I believe I eclipsed myself. Words that I did not know I had ever heard of seemed to come pouring out of my open mouth.

'"When we get you past," whispered Bill, "you'll howl louder; you'll howl louder when we're burning your feet off."

'I screamed in my terror those awful songs of joy. In all the nightmares that men have ever dreamed, there has never been anything so blighting and horrible as the faces of those five men, looking out of their poke-bonnets; the figures of district visitors with the faces of devils. I cannot think there is anything so heart-breaking in hell.

'For a sickening instant I thought that the bustle of my companions and the perfect respectability of all our dresses would overcome the policeman and induce him to let us pass. He wavered, so far as one can describe anything so solid as a policeman as wavering. I lurched suddenly forward and ran my head into his chest, calling out (if I remember correctly), "Oh, crikey, blimey, Bill." It was at that moment that I remembered most dearly that I was the Vicar of Chuntsey, in Essex.

'My desperate coup saved me. The policeman had me hard by the back of the neck.

'"You come along with me," he began, but Bill cut in with his perfect imitation of a lady's finnicking voice.

'"Oh, pray, constable, don't make a disturbance with our poor friend. We will get her quietly home. She does drink too much, but she is quite a lady—only eccentric."

'"She butted me in the stomach," said the policeman briefly.

'"Eccentricities of genius," said Sam earnestly.

'"Pray let me take her home," reiterated Bill, in the resumed character of Miss James, "she wants looking after." "She does," said the policeman, "but I'll look after her."

'"That's no good," cried Bill feverishly. "She wants her friends. She wants a particular medicine we've got."

'"Yes," assented Miss Mowbray, with excitement, "no other medicine any good, constable. Complaint quite unique."

'"I'm all righ'. Cutchy, cutchy, coo!" remarked, to his eternal shame, the Vicar of Chuntsey.

'"Look here, ladies," said the constable sternly, "I don't like the eccentricity of your friend, and I don't like 'er songs, or 'er 'ead in my stomach. And now I come to think of it, I don't like the looks of you I've seen many as quiet dressed as you as was wrong 'uns. Who are you?"

'"We've not our cards with us," said Miss Mowbray, with indescribable dignity. "Nor do we see why we should be insulted by any Jack-in-office who chooses to be rude to ladies, when he is paid to protect them. If you choose to take advantage of the weakness of our unfortunate friend, no doubt you are legally entitled to take her. But if you fancy you have any legal right to bully us, you will find yourself in the wrong box."

'The truth and dignity of this staggered the policeman for a moment. Under cover of their advantage my five persecutors turned for an instant on me faces like faces of the damned and then swished off into the darkness. When the constable first turned his lantern and his suspicions on to them, I had seen the telegraphic look flash from face to face saying that only retreat was possible now.

'By this time I was sinking slowly to the pavement, in a state of acute reflection. So long as the ruffians were with me, I dared not quit the role of drunkard. For if I had begun to talk reasonably and explain the real case, the officer would merely have thought that I was slightly recovered and would have put me in charge of my friends. Now, however, if I liked I might safely undeceive him.

'But I confess I did not like. The chances of life are many, and it may doubtless sometimes lie in the narrow path of duty for a clergyman of the Church of England to pretend to be a drunken old woman; but such necessities are, I imagine, sufficiently rare to appear to many improbable. Suppose the story got about that I had pretended to be drunk. Suppose people did not all think it was pretence!

'I lurched up, the policeman half-lifting me. I went along weakly and quietly for about a hundred yards. The officer evidently thought that I was too sleepy and feeble to effect an escape, and so held me lightly and easily enough. Past one turning, two turnings, three turnings, four turnings, he trailed me with him, a limp and slow and reluctant figure. At the fourth turning, I suddenly broke from his hand and tore down the street like a maddened stag. He was unprepared, he was heavy, and it was dark. I ran and ran and ran, and in five minutes' running, found I was gaining. In half an hour I was out in the fields under the holy and blessed stars, where I tore off my accursed shawl and bonnet and buried them in clean earth.'

The old gentleman had finished his story and leant back in his chair. Both the matter and the manner of his narration had, as time went on, impressed me favourably. He was an old duffer and pedant, but behind these things he was a country-bred man and gentleman, and had showed courage and a sporting instinct in the hour of desperation. He had told his story with many quaint formalities of diction, but also with a very convincing realism.

'And now—' I began.

'And now,' said Shorter, leaning forward again with something like servile energy, 'and now, Mr Swinburne, what about that unhappy man Hawker. I cannot tell what those men meant, or how far what they said was real. But surely there is danger. I cannot go to the police, for reasons that you perceive. Among other things, they wouldn't believe me. What is to be done?'

I took out my watch. It was already half past twelve.

'My friend Basil Grant,' I said, 'is the best man we can go to. He and I were to have gone to the same dinner tonight; but he will just have come back by now. Have you any objection to taking a cab?'

'Not at all,' he replied, rising politely, and gathering up his absurd plaid shawl.

A rattle in a hansom brought us underneath the sombre pile of workmen's flats in Lambeth which Grant inhabited; a climb up a wearisome wooden staircase brought us to his garret. When I entered that wooden and scrappy interior, the white gleam of Basil's shirt-front and the lustre of his fur coat flung on the wooden settle, struck me as a contrast. He was drinking a glass of wine before retiring. I was right; he had come back from the dinner-party.

He listened to the repetition of the story of the Rev. Ellis Shorter with the genuine simplicity and respect which he never failed to exhibit in dealing with any human being. When it was over he said simply:

'Do you know a man named Captain Fraser?'

I was so startled at this totally irrelevant reference to the worthy collector of chimpanzees with whom I ought to have dined that evening, that I glanced sharply at Grant. The result was that I did not look at Mr Shorter. I only heard him answer, in his most nervous tone, 'No.'

Basil, however, seemed to find something very curious about his answer or his demeanour generally, for he kept his big blue eyes fixed on the old clergyman, and though the eyes were quite quiet they stood out more and more from his head.

'You are quite sure, Mr Shorter,' he repeated, 'that you don't know Captain Fraser?'

'Quite,' answered the vicar, and I was certainly puzzled to find him returning so much to the timidity, not to say the demoralization, of his tone when he first entered my presence.

Basil sprang smartly to his feet.

'Then our course is clear,' he said. 'You have not even begun your investigation, my dear Mr Shorter; the first thing for us to do is to go together to see Captain Fraser.'

'When?' asked the clergyman, stammering.

'Now,' said Basil, putting one arm in his fur coat.

The old clergyman rose to his feet, quaking all over.

'I really do not think that it is necessary,' he said.

Basil took his arm out of the fur coat, threw it over the chair again, and put his hands in his pockets.

'Oh,' he said, with emphasis. 'Oh—you don't think it necessary; then,' and he added the words with great clearness and deliberation, 'then, Mr Ellis Shorter, I can only say that I would like to see you without your whiskers.'

And at these words I also rose to my feet, for the great tragedy of my life had come. Splendid and exciting as life was in continual contact with an intellect like Basil's, I had always the feeling that that splendour and excitement were on the borderland of sanity. He lived perpetually near the vision of the reason of things which makes men lose their reason. And I felt of his insanity as men feel of the death of friends with heart disease. It might come anywhere, in a field, in a hansom cab, looking at a sunset, smoking a cigarette. It had come now. At the very moment of delivering a judgement for the salvation of a fellow creature, Basil Grant had gone mad.

'Your whiskers,' he cried, advancing with blazing eyes. 'Give me your whiskers. And your bald head.'

The old vicar naturally retreated a step or two. I stepped between.

'Sit down, Basil,' I implored, 'you're a little excited. Finish your wine.'

'Whiskers,' he answered sternly, 'whiskers.'

And with that he made a dash at the old gentleman, who made a dash for the door, but was intercepted. And then, before I knew where I was the quiet room was turned into something between a pantomime and a pandemonium by those two. Chairs were flung over with a crash, tables were vaulted with a noise like thunder, screens were smashed, crockery scattered in smithereens, and still Basil Grant bounded and bellowed after the Rev. Ellis Shorter.

And now I began to perceive something else, which added the last half-witted touch to my mystification. The Rev. Ellis Shorter, of Chuntsey, in Essex, was by no means behaving as I had previously noticed him to behave, or as, considering his age and station, I should have expected him to behave. His power of dodging, leaping, and fighting would have been amazing in a lad of seventeen, and in this doddering old vicar looked like a sort of farcical fairy-tale. Moreover, he did not seem to be so much astonished as I had thought. There was even a look of something like enjoyment in his eyes; so there was in the eye of Basil. In fact, the unintelligible truth must be told. They were both laughing.

At length Shorter was cornered.

'Come, come, Mr Grant,' he panted, 'you can't do anything to me. It's quite legal. And it doesn't do any one the least harm. It's only a social fiction. A result of our complex society, Mr Grant.'

'I don't blame you, my man,' said Basil coolly. 'But I want your whiskers. And your bald head. Do they belong to Captain Fraser?'

'No, no,' said Mr Shorter, laughing, 'we provide them ourselves. They don't belong to Captain Fraser.'

'What the deuce does all this mean?' I almost screamed. 'Are you all in an infernal nightmare? Why should Mr Shorter's bald head belong to Captain Fraser? How could it? What the deuce has Captain Fraser to do with the affair? What is the matter with him? You dined with him, Basil.'

'No,' said Grant, 'I didn't.'

'Didn't you go to Mrs Thornton's dinner-party?' I asked, staring. 'Why not?'

'Well,' said Basil, with a slow and singular smile, 'the fact is I was detained by a visitor. I have him, as a point of fact, in my bedroom.'

'In your bedroom?' I repeated; but my imagination had reached that point when he might have said in his coal scuttle or his waistcoat pocket.

Grant stepped to the door of an inner room, flung it open and walked in. Then he came out again with the last of the bodily wonders of that wild night. He introduced into the sitting-room, in an apologetic manner, and by the nape of the neck, a limp clergyman with a bald head, white whiskers and a plaid shawl.

'Sit down, gentlemen,' cried Grant, striking his hands heartily. 'Sit down all of you and have a glass of wine. As you say, there is no harm in it, and if Captain Fraser had simply dropped me a hint I could have saved him from dropping a good sum of money. Not that you would have liked that, eh?'

The two duplicate clergymen, who were sipping their Burgundy with two duplicate grins, laughed heartily at this, and one of them carelessly pulled off his whiskers and laid them on the table.

'Basil,' I said, 'if you are my friend, save me. What is all this?'

He laughed again.

'Only another addition, Cherub, to your collection of Queer Trades. These two gentlemen (whose health I have now the pleasure of drinking) are Professional Detainers.'

'And what on earth's that?' I asked.

'It's really very simple, Mr Swinburne,' began he who had once been the Rev. Ellis Shorter, of Chuntsey, in Essex; and it gave me a shock indescribable to hear out of that pompous and familiar form come no longer its own pompous and familiar voice, but the brisk sharp tones of a young city man. 'It is really nothing very important. We are paid by our clients to detain in conversation, on some harmless pretext, people whom they want out of the way for a few hours. And Captain Fraser—' and with that he hesitated and smiled.

Basil smiled also. He intervened.

'The fact is that Captain Fraser, who is one of my best friends, wanted us both out of the way very much. He is sailing tonight for East Africa, and the lady with whom we were all to have dined is—er—what is I believe described as "the romance of his life". He wanted that two hours with her, and employed these two reverend gentlemen to detain us at our houses so as to let him have the field to himself.'

'And of course,' said the late Mr Shorter apologetically to me, 'as I had to keep a gentleman at home from keeping an appointment with a lady, I had to come with something rather hot and strong—rather urgent. It wouldn't have done to be tame.'

'Oh,' I said, 'I acquit you of tameness.'

'Thank you, sir,' said the man respectfully, 'always very grateful for any recommendation, sir.'

The other man idly pushed back his artificial bald head, revealing close red hair, and spoke dreamily, perhaps under the influence of Basil's admirable Burgundy.

'It's wonderful how common it's getting, gentlemen. Our office is busy from morning till night. I've no doubt you've often knocked up against us before. You just take notice. When an old bachelor goes on boring you with hunting stories, when you're burning to be introduced to somebody, he's from our bureau. When a lady calls on parish work and stops hours, just when you wanted to go to the Robinsons', she's from our bureau. The Robinson hand, sir, may be darkly seen.'

'There is one thing I don't understand,' I said. 'Why you are both vicars.'

A shade crossed the brow of the temporary incumbent of Chuntsey, in Essex.

'That may have been a mistake, sir,' he said. 'But it was not our fault. It was all the munificence of Captain Fraser. He requested that the highest price and talent on our tariff should be employed to detain you gentlemen. Now the highest payment in our office goes to those who impersonate vicars, as being the most respectable and more of a strain. We are paid five guineas a visit. We have had the good fortune to satisfy the firm with our work; and we are now permanently vicars. Before that we had two years as colonels, the next in our scale. Colonels are four guineas.'

3

THE BLUE CROSS

Between the silver ribbon of morning and the green glittering ribbon of sea, the boat touched Harwich and let loose a swarm of folk like flies, among whom the man we must follow was by no means conspicuous—nor wished to be. There was nothing notable about him, except a slight contrast between the holiday gaiety of his clothes and the official gravity of his face. His clothes included a slight, pale grey jacket, a white waistcoat, and a silver straw hat with a grey-blue ribbon. His lean face was dark by contrast, and ended in a curt black beard that looked Spanish and suggested an Elizabethan ruff. He was smoking a cigarette with the seriousness of an idler. There was nothing about him to indicate the fact that the grey jacket covered a loaded revolver, that the white waistcoat covered a police cord, or that the straw hat covered one of the most powerful intellects in Europe. For this was Valentin himself, the head of the Paris police and the most famous investigator of the world; and he was coming from Brussels to London to make the greatest arrest of the century.

Flambeau was in England. The police of three countries had tracked the great criminal at last from Ghent to Brussels, from Brussels to the Hook of Holland; and it was conjectured that he would take some advantage of the unfamiliarity and confusion of the Eucharistic Congress, then taking place in London. Probably he would travel as some minor clerk or secretary connected with it; but, of course, Valentin could not be certain; nobody could be certain about Flambeau.

It is many years now since this colossus of crime suddenly ceased keeping the world in a turmoil; and when he ceased, as they said after the death of Roland, there was a great quiet upon the earth. But in his best days (I mean, of course, his worst) Flambeau was a figure as statuesque and international as the Kaiser. Almost every morning the daily paper announced that he had escaped the consequences of one extraordinary crime by committing another. He was a Gascon of gigantic stature and bodily daring; and the wildest tales were told of his outbursts of athletic humour; how he turned the juge d'instruction upside down and stood him on his head, 'to clear his mind'; how he ran down the Rue de Rivoli with a policeman under each arm. It is due to him to say that his fantastic physical strength was generally employed in such bloodless though undignified scenes; his real crimes were chiefly those of ingenious and wholesale robbery. But each of his thefts was almost a new sin, and would make a story by itself. It was he who ran the great Tyrolean Dairy Company in London, with no dairies, no cows, no carts, no milk, but with some thousand subscribers. These he served by the simple operation of moving the little milk-cans outside people's doors to the doors of his own customers. It was he who had kept up an unaccountable and close correspondence with a young lady whose whole letter-bag was intercepted, by the extraordinary trick of photographing his messages infinitesimally small upon the slides of a microscope. A sweeping simplicity, however, marked many of his experiments. It is said he once repainted all the numbers in a street in the dead of night merely to divert one traveller into a trap. It is quite certain that he invented a portable pillar-box, which he put up at corners in quiet suburbs on the chance of strangers dropping postal orders into it. Lastly he was known to be a startling acrobat; despite his huge figure, he could leap like a grasshopper and melt into the treetops like a monkey. Hence the great Valentin, when he set out to find Flambeau, was perfectly well aware that his adventures would not end when he had found him.

But how was he to find him? On this the great Valentin's ideas were still in process of settlement.

There was one thing which Flambeau, with all his dexterity of disguise, could not cover, and that was his singular height. If Valentin's quick eye had caught a tall apple-woman, a tall grenadier, or even a tolerably tall duchess, he might have arrested them on the spot. But all along his train there was nobody that could be a disguised Flambeau, any more than a cat could be a disguised giraffe. About the people on the boat he had already satisfied himself; and the people picked up at Harwich or on the journey limited themselves with certainty to six. There was a short railway official travelling up to the terminus, three fairly short market-gardeners picked up two stations afterwards, one very short widow lady going up from a small Essex town, and a very short Roman Catholic priest going up from a small Essex village. When it came to the last case, Valentin gave it up and almost laughed. The little priest was so much the essence of those Eastern flats: he had a face as round and dull as a Norfolk dumpling; he had eyes as empty as the North Sea; he had several brown-paper parcels which he was quite incapable of collecting. The Eucharistic Congress had doubtless sucked out of their local stagnation many such creatures, blind and helpless, like moles disinterred. Valentin was a sceptic in the severe style of France, and could have no love for priests. But he could have pity for them, and this one might have provoked pity in anybody. He had a large, shabby umbrella, which constantly fell on the floor. He did not seem to know which was the right end of his return ticket. He explained with a moon-calf simplicity to everybody in the carriage that he had to be careful, because he had something made of real silver 'with blue stones' in one of his brown-paper parcels. His quaint blending of Essex flatness with saintly simplicity continuously amused the Frenchman till the priest arrived (somehow) at Stratford with all his parcels, and came back for his umbrella. When he did the last, Valentin even had the good nature to warn him not to take care of the silver by telling everybody about it. But to whomever he talked, Valentin kept his eye open for someone else; he looked out steadily for anyone, rich or poor, male or female, who was well up to six feet; for Flambeau was four inches above it.

He alighted at Liverpool Street, however, quite conscientiously secure that he had not missed the criminal so far. He then went to Scotland Yard to regularize his position and arrange for help in case of need; he then lit another cigarette and went for a long stroll in the streets of London. As he was walking in the streets and squares beyond Victoria, he paused suddenly and stood. It was a quaint, quiet square, very typical of London, full of an accidental stillness. The tall, flat houses round looked at once prosperous and uninhabited; the square of shrubbery in the center looked as deserted as a green Pacific islet. One of the four sides was much higher than the rest, like a dais; and the line of this side was broken by one of London's admirable accidents—a restaurant that looked as if it had strayed from Soho. It was an unreasonably attractive object, with dwarf plants in pots and long, striped blinds of lemon yellow and white. It stood specially high above the street, and in the usual patchwork way of London, a flight of steps from the street ran up to a first-floor window. Valentin stood and smoked in front of the yellow-white blinds and considered them long.

The most incredible thing about miracles is that they happen. A few clouds in heaven do come together into the staring shape of one human eye. A tree does stand up in the landscape of a doubtful journey in the exact and elaborate shape of a note of interrogation. I have seen both these things myself within the last few days. Nelson does die in the instant of victory; and a man named Williams does quite accidentally murder a man named Williamson; it sounds like a sort of infanticide. In short, there is in life an element of elfin coincidence which people reckoning on the prosaic may perpetually miss. As it has been well expressed in the paradox of Poe, wisdom should reckon on the unforeseen.

Aristide Valentin was unfathomably French; and the French intelligence is intelligence specially and solely. He was not 'a thinking machine'; for that is a brainless phrase of modern fatalism and materialism. A machine only is a machine because it cannot think. But he was a thinking man, and a plain man at the same time. All his wonderful successes, that looked like conjuring, had been gained by plodding logic, by clear and commonplace French thought. The French electrify the world not by starting any paradox, they electrify it by carrying out a truism. They carry a truism so far—as in the French Revolution. But exactly because Valentin understood reason, he understood the limits of reason. Only a man who knows nothing of motors talks of motoring without petrol; only a man who knows nothing of reason talks of reasoning without strong, undisputed first principles. Here he had no strong first principles. Flambeau had been missed at Harwich; and if he was in London at all, he might be anything from a tall tramp on Wimbledon Common to a tall toast-master at the Hotel Metropole. In such a naked state of nescience, Valentin had a view and a method of his own.

In such cases he reckoned on the unforeseen. In such cases, when he could not follow the train of the reasonable, he coldly and carefully followed the train of the unreasonable. Instead of going to the right places—banks, police-stations, rendezvous—

he systematically went to the wrong places; knocked at every empty house, turned down every cul de sac, went up every lane blocked with rubbish, went round every crescent that led him uselessly out of the way. He defended this crazy course quite logically. He said that if one had a clue this was the worst way; but if one had no clue at all it was the best, because there was just the chance that any oddity that caught the eye of the pursuer might be the same that had caught the eye of the pursued. Somewhere a man must begin, and it had better be just where another man might stop. Something about that flight of steps up to the shop, something about the quietude and quaintness of the restaurant, roused all the detective's rare romantic fancy and made him resolve to strike at random. He went up the steps, and, sitting down by the window, asked for a cup of black coffee.

It was half-way through the morning, and he had not breakfasted; the slight litter of other breakfasts stood about on the table to remind him of his hunger; and, adding a poached egg to his order, he proceeded musingly to shake some white sugar into his coffee, thinking all the time about Flambeau. He remembered how Flambeau had escaped, once by a pair of nail scissors, and once by a house on fire; once by having to pay for an unstamped letter, and once by getting people to look through a telescope at a comet that might destroy the world. He thought his detective brain as good as the criminal's, which was true. But he fully realized the disadvantage. 'The criminal is the creative artist; the detective only the critic,' he said with a sour smile, and lifted his coffee cup to his lips slowly, and put it down very quickly. He had put salt in it.

He looked at the vessel from which the silvery powder had come; it was certainly a sugar-basin; as unmistakably meant for sugar as a champagne-bottle for champagne. He wondered why they should keep salt in it. He looked to see if there were any more orthodox vessels. Yes, there were two salt-cellars quite full. Perhaps there was some specialty in the condiment in the salt-cellars. He tasted it; it was sugar. Then he looked round at the restaurant with a refreshed air of interest, to see if there were any other traces of that singular artistic taste which puts the sugar in the salt-cellars and the salt in the sugar-basin. Except for an odd splash of some dark fluid on one of the white-papered walls, the whole place appeared neat, cheerful, and ordinary. He rang the bell for the waiter.

When that official hurried up, fuzzy-haired and somewhat blear-eyed at that early hour, the detective (who was not without an appreciation of the simpler forms of humour) asked him to taste the sugar and see if it was up to the high reputation of the hotel. The result was that the waiter yawned suddenly and woke up.

'Do you play this delicate joke on your customers every morning?' inquired Valentin. 'Does changing the salt and sugar never pall on you as a jest?'

The waiter, when this irony grew clearer, stammeringly assured him that the establishment had certainly no such intention; it must be a most curious mistake. He picked up the sugar-basin and looked at it; he picked up the salt-cellar and looked at that, his face growing more and more bewildered. At last he abruptly excused himself, and hurrying away, returned in a few seconds with the proprietor. The proprietor also examined the sugar-basin and then the salt-cellar; the proprietor also looked bewildered.

Suddenly the waiter seemed to grow inarticulate with a rush of words.

'I zink,' he stuttered eagerly, 'I zink it is those two clergymen.'
'What two clergymen?'
'The two clergymen,' said the waiter, 'that threw soup at the wall.'

'Threw soup at the wall?' repeated Valentin, feeling sure this must be some Italian metaphor.

'Yes, yes,' said the attendant excitedly, and pointing at the dark splash on the white paper; 'threw it over there on the wall.'

Valentin looked his query at the proprietor, who came to his rescue with fuller reports.

'Yes, sir,' he said, 'it's quite true, though I don't suppose it has anything to do with the sugar and salt. Two clergymen came in and drank soup here very early, as soon as the shutters were taken down. They were both very quiet, respectable people; one of them paid the bill and went out; the other, who seemed a slower coach altogether, was some minutes longer getting his things together. But he went at last. Only, the instant before he stepped into the street he deliberately picked up his cup, which he had only half emptied, and threw the soup slap on the wall. I was in the back room myself, and so was the waiter; so I could only rush out in time to find the wall splashed and the shop empty. It didn't do any particular damage, but it was confounded cheek; and I tried to catch the men in the street. They were too far off though; I only noticed they went round the corner into Carstairs Street.'

The detective was on his feet, hat settled and stick in hand. He had already decided that in the universal darkness of his mind he could only follow the first odd finger that pointed; and this finger was odd enough. Paying his bill and clashing the glass doors behind him, he was soon swinging round into the other street.

It was fortunate that even in such fevered moments his eye was cool and quick. Something in a shop-front went by him like a mere flash; yet he went back to look at it. The shop was a popular greengrocer and fruiterer's, an array of goods set out in the open air and plainly ticketed with their names and prices. In the two most prominent compartments were two heaps, of oranges and of nuts respectively. On the heap of nuts lay a scrap of cardboard, on which was written in bold, blue chalk, 'Best tangerine oranges, two a penny.' On the oranges was the equally clear and exact description, 'Finest Brazil nuts, 4d. a lb.' M. Valentin looked at these two placards and fancied he had met this highly subtle form of humour before, and that somewhat recently. He drew the attention of the red-faced fruiterer, who was looking rather sullenly up and down the street, to this inaccuracy in his advertisements. The fruiterer said nothing, but sharply put each card into its proper place. The detective, leaning elegantly on his walking-cane, continued to scrutinize the shop. At last he said: 'Pray excuse my apparent irrelevance, my good sir, but I should like to ask you a question in experimental psychology and the association of ideas.'

The red-faced shopman regarded him with an eye of menace; but he continued gaily, swinging his cane. 'Why,' he pursued, 'why are two tickets wrongly placed in a greengrocer's shop like a shovel hat that has come to London for a holiday? Or in case I do not make myself clear, what is the mystical association which connects the idea of nuts marked as oranges with the idea of two clergymen, one tall and the other short?'

The eyes of the tradesman stood out of his head like a snail's; he really seemed for an instant likely to fling himself upon the stranger. At last he stammered angrily: 'I don't know what you 'ave to do with it, but if you're one of their friends, you can tell 'em from me that I'll knock their silly 'eads off, parsons or no parsons, if they upset my apples again.'

'Indeed?' asked the detective, with great sympathy. 'Did they upset your apples?'

'One of 'em did,' said the heated shopman; 'rolled 'em all over the street. I'd 'ave caught the fool but for havin' to pick 'em up.'

'Which way did these parsons go?' asked Valentin.

'Up that second road on the left-hand side, and then across the square,' said the other promptly.

'Thanks,' said Valentin, and vanished like a fairy. On the other side of the second square he found a policeman, and said: 'This is urgent, constable; have you seen two clergymen in shovel hats?'

The policeman began to chuckle heavily. 'I 'ave, sir; and if you arst me, one of 'em was drunk. He stood in the middle of the road that bewildered that—'

'Which way did they go?' snapped Valentin.

'They took one of them yellow buses over there,' answered the man; 'them that go to Hampstead.'

Valentin produced his official card and said very rapidly: 'Call up two of your men to come with me in pursuit,' and crossed the road with such contagious energy that the ponderous policeman was moved to almost agile obedience. In a minute and a half the French detective was joined on the opposite pavement by an inspector and a man in plain clothes.

'Well, sire,' began the former, with smiling importance, 'and what may—?'

Valentin pointed suddenly with his cane. 'I'll tell you on the top of that omnibus,' he said, and was darting and dodging across the tangle of the traffic. When all three sank panting on the top seats of the yellow vehicle, the inspector said: 'We could go four times as quick in a taxi.'

'Quite true,' replied their leader placidly, 'if we only had an idea of where we were going.'

'Well, where are you going?' asked the other, staring.

Valentin smoked frowningly for a few seconds; then, removing his cigarette, he said: 'If you know what a man's doing, get in front of him; but if you want to guess what he's doing, keep behind him. Stray when he strays; stop when he stops; travel as slowly as he. Then you may see what he saw and may act as he acted. All we can do is to keep our eyes skinned for a queer thing.'

'What sort of a queer thing do you mean?' asked the inspector.

'Any sort of queer thing,' answered Valentin, and relapsed into obstinate silence.

The yellow omnibus crawled up the northern roads for what seemed like hours on end; the great detective would not explain further, and perhaps his assistants felt a silent and growing doubt of his errand. Perhaps, also, they felt a silent and growing desire for lunch, for the hours crept long past the normal luncheon hour, and the long roads of the North London suburbs seemed to shoot out into length after length like an infernal telescope. It was one of those journeys on which a man perpetually feels that now at last he must have come to the end of the universe, and then finds he has only come to the beginning of Tufnell Park. London died away in draggled taverns and dreary scrubs, and then was unaccountably born again in blazing high streets and blatant hotels. It was like passing through thirteen separate vulgar cities all just touching each other. But though the winter twilight was already threatening the road ahead of them, the Parisian detective still sat silent and watchful, eyeing the frontage of the streets that slid by on either side. By the time they had left Camden Town behind, the policemen were nearly asleep; at least, they gave something like a jump as Valentin leapt erect, struck a hand on each man's shoulder, and shouted to the driver to stop.

They tumbled down the steps into the road without realizing why they had been dislodged; when they looked round for enlightenment they found Valentin triumphantly pointing his finger towards a window on the left side of the road. It was a large window, forming part of the long facade of a gilt and palatial public-house; it was the part reserved for respectable dining, and labelled 'Restaurant.' This window, like all the rest along the frontage of the hotel, was of frosted and figured glass, but in the middle of it was a big, black smash, like a star in the ice.

'Our cue at last,' cried Valentin, waving his stick; 'the place with the broken window.'

'What window? What cue?' asked his principal assistant. 'Why, what proof is there that this has anything to do with them?'

Valentin almost broke his bamboo stick with rage.

'Proof!' he cried. 'Good God! the man is looking for proof! Why, of course, the chances are twenty to one that it has nothing to do with them. But what else can we do? Don't you see we must either follow one wild possibility or else go home to bed?' He banged his way into the restaurant, followed by his companions, and they were soon seated at a late luncheon at a little table, and looking at the star of smashed glass from the inside. Not that it was very informative to them even then.

'Got your window broken, I see,' said Valentin to the waiter, as he paid his bill.

'Yes, sir,' answered the attendant, bending busily over the change, to which Valentin silently added an enormous tip. The waiter straightened himself with mild but unmistakable animation.

'Ah, yes, sir,' he said. 'Very odd thing, that, sir.'

'Indeed? Tell us about it,' said the detective with careless curiosity.

'Well, two gents in black came in,' said the waiter; 'two of those foreign parsons that are running about. They had a cheap and quiet little lunch, and one of them paid for it and went out. The other was just going out to join him when I looked at my change again and found he'd paid me more than three times too much. "Here," I say to the chap who was nearly out of the door, "you've paid too much." "Oh," he says, very cool, "have we?" "Yes," I says, and picks up the bill to show him. Well, that was a knockout.'

'What do you mean?' asked his interlocutor.

'Well, I'd have sworn on seven Bibles that I'd put 4s. on that bill. But now I saw I'd put 14s., as plain as paint.'

'Well?' cried Valentin, moving slowly, but with burning eyes, 'and then?'

'The parson at the door he says, all serene, "Sorry to confuse your accounts, but it'll pay for the window." "What window?" I says. "The one I'm going to break," he says, and smashed that blessed pane with his umbrella.'

All the inquirers made an exclamation; and the inspector said under his breath: 'Are we after escaped lunatics?' The waiter went on with some relish for the ridiculous story:

'I was so knocked silly for a second, I couldn't do anything. The man marched out of the place and joined his friend just round the corner. Then they went so quick up Bullock Street that I couldn't catch them, though I ran round the bars to do it.'

'Bullock Street,' said the detective, and shot up that thoroughfare as quickly as the strange couple he pursued.

Their journey now took them through bare brick ways like tunnels; streets that seemed built out of the blank backs of everything and everywhere. Dusk was deepening, and it was not easy even for the London policemen to guess in what exact direction they were treading. The inspector, however, was pretty certain that they would eventually strike some part of Hampstead Heath. Abruptly one bulging and gas-lit window broke the blue twilight like a bull's-eye lantern; and Valentin stopped an instant before a little garish sweet-stuff shop. After an instant's hesitate he went in; he stood amid the gaudy colours of the confectionary with entire gravity and bought thirteen chocolate cigars with a certain care. He was clearly preparing an opening; but he did not need one.

An angular, elderly young woman in the shop had regarded his pleasant appearance with a merely automatic inquiry; but when she saw the door behind him blocked with the blue uniform of the inspector, her eyes seemed to wake up.

'Oh,' she said, 'if you've come about that parcel, I've sent it off already.'

'Parcel!' repeated Valentin; and it was his turn to look inquiring.

'I mean the parcel the gentleman left—the clergyman gentleman.'

'For goodness' sake,' said Valentin, leaning forward with his first real confession of eagerness, 'for Heaven's sake tell us what happened exactly.'

'Well,' said the woman, a little doubtfully, 'the clergymen came in about half an hour ago and bought some peppermints and talked a bit, and then went off towards the Heath. But a second after, one of them runs back into the shop and says, "Have I left a parcel?" Well, I looked everywhere and couldn't see one; so he says, "Never mind; but if it should turn up, please post it to this address," and he left me the address and a shilling for my trouble. And sure enough, though I thought I'd looked everywhere, I found he'd left a brown-paper parcel, so I posted it to the place he said. I can't remember the address now; it was somewhere in Westminster. But as the thing seemed so important, I thought perhaps the police had come about it.'

'So they have,' said Valentin shortly. 'Is Hampstead Heath near here?'

'Straight on for fifteen minutes,' said the woman, 'and you'll come right out on the open.' Valentin sprang out of the shop and began to run. The other detectives followed him at a reluctant trot.

The street they threaded was so narrow and shut in by

shadows that when they came out unexpectedly into the void common and vast sky they were startled to find the evening still so light and clear. A perfect dome of peacock-green sank into gold amid the blackening trees and the dark violet distances. The glowing green tint was just deep enough to pick out in points of crystal one or two stars. All that was left of the daylight lay in a golden glitter across the edge of Hampstead and that popular hollow which is called the Vale of Health. The holiday-makers who roam this region had not wholly dispersed: a few couples sat shapelessly on benches; and here and there a distant girl still shrieked in one of the swings. The glory of heaven deepened and darkened around the sublime vulgarity of man; and standing on the slope and looking across the valley, Valentin beheld the thing which he sought.

Among the black and breaking groups in that distance was one especially black which did not break—a group of two figures clerically clad. Though they seemed as small as insects, Valentin could see that one of them was much smaller than the other. Though the other had a student's stoop and an inconspicuous manner, he could see that the man was well over six feet high. He shut his teeth and went forward, whirling his stick impatiently. By the time he had substantially diminished the distance and magnified the two black figures as in a vast microscope, he had perceived something else; something which startled him, and yet which he had somehow expected. Whoever was the tall priest, thee could be no doubt about the identity of the short one. It was his friend of the Harwich train, the stumpy little cure of Essex whom he had warned about his brown-paper parcels.

Now, so far as this went, everything fitted in finally and rationally enough. Valentin had learned by his inquiries that morning that a Father Brown from Essex was bringing up a silver cross with sapphires, a relic of considerable value, to show some of the foreign priests at the congress. This undoubtedly was the 'silver with blue stones'; and Father Brown undoubtedly was the little greenhorn in the train. Now there was nothing wonderful about the fact that what Valentin had found out Flambeau had also found out; Flambeau found out everything. Also there was nothing wonderful in the fact that when Flambeau heard of a sapphire cross he should try to steal it; that was the most natural thing in all natural history. And most certainly there was nothing wonderful about the fact that Flambeau should have it all his own way with such a silly sheep as the man with the umbrella and the parcels. He was the sort of man whom anybody could lead on a string to the North Pole; it was not surprising that an actor like Flambeau, dressed as another priest, could lead him to Hampstead Heath. So far the crime seemed clear enough; and while the detective pitied the priest for his helplessness, he almost despised Flambeau for condescending to so gullible a victim. But when Valentin thought of all that had happened in between, of all that had led him to his triumph, he racked his brains for the smallest rhyme or reason in it. What had the stealing of a blue-and-silver cross from a priest from Essex to do with chucking soup at wallpaper? What had it to do with calling nuts oranges, or with paying for windows first and breaking them afterwards? He had come to the end of his chase; yet somehow he had missed the middle of it. When he failed (which was seldom), he had usually grasped the clue, but nevertheless missed the criminal. Here he had grasped the criminal, but still he could not grasp the clue.

The two figures that they followed were crawling like black flies across the huge green contour of a hill. They were evidently sunk in conversation, and perhaps did not notice where they were going; but they were certainly going to the wilder and more silent heights of the Heath. As their pursuers gained on them, the latter had to use the undignified attitudes of the deer-stalker, to crouch behind clumps of trees and even to crawl prostrate in deep grass. By these ungainly ingenuities the hunters even came close enough to the quarry to hear the murmur of the discussion, but no word could be distinguished except the word 'reason' recurring frequently in a high and almost childish voice. Once, over an abrupt dip of land and a dense tangle of thickets, the detectives actually lost the two figures they were following. They did not find the trail again for an agonizing ten minutes, and then it led round the brow of a great dome of hill overlooking an amphitheatre of rich and desolate sunset scenery. Under a tree in this commanding yet neglected spot was an old ramshackle wooden seat. On this seat sat the two priests still in serious speech together. The gorgeous green and gold still clung to the darkening horizon; but the dome above was turning slowly from peacock-green to peacock-blue, and the stars detached themselves more and more like solid jewels. Mutely motioning to his followers, Valentin contrived to creep up behind the big branching tree, and, standing there in deathly silence, heard the words of the strange priests for the first time.

After he had listened for a minute and a half, he was gripped by a devilish doubt. Perhaps he had dragged the two English policemen to the wastes of a nocturnal heath on an errand no saner than seeking figs on thistles. For the two priests were talking exactly like priests, piously, with learning and leisure, about the most aerial enigmas of theology. The little Essex priest spoke the more simply, with his round face turned to the strengthening stars; the other talked with his head bowed, as if he were not even worthy to look at them. But no more innocently clerical conversation could have been heard in any white Italian cloister or black Spanish cathedral.

The first he heard was the tail of one of Father Brown's

sentences, which ended: '...what they really meant in the Middle Ages by the heavens being incorruptible.'

The taller priest nodded his bowed head and said:

'Ah, yes, these modern infidels appeal to their reason; but who can look at those millions of worlds and not feel that there may well be wonderful universes above us where reason is utterly unreasonable?'

'No,' said the other priest; 'reason is always reasonable, even in the last limbo, in the lost borderland of things. I know that people charge the Church with lowering reason, but it is just the other way. Alone on earth, the Church makes reason really supreme. Alone on earth, the Church affirms that God Himself is bound by reason.'

The other priest raised his austere face to the spangled sky and said:

'Yet who knows if in that infinite universe—?'

'Only infinite physically,' said the little priest, turning sharply in his seat, 'not infinite in the sense of escaping from the laws of truth.'

Valentin behind his tree was tearing his finger-nails with silent fury. He seemed almost to hear the sniggers of the English detectives whom he had brought so far on a fantastic guess only to listen to the metaphysical gossip of two mild old parsons. In his impatience he lost the equally elaborate answer of the tall cleric, and when he listened again it was again Father Brown who was speaking:

'Reason and justice grip the remotest and the loneliest star. Look at those stars. Don't they look as if they were single diamonds and sapphires? Well, you can imagine any mad botany or geology you please. Think of forests of adamant with leaves of brilliants. Think the moon is a blue moon, a single elephantine sapphire. But don't fancy that all that frantic astronomy would make the smallest difference to the reason and justice of conduct.

On plains of opal, under cliffs cut out of pearl, you would still find a notice-board, "Thou shalt not steal."'

Valentin was just in the act of rising from his rigid and crouching attitude and creeping away as softly as might be, felled by the one great folly of his life. But something in the very silence of the tall priest made him stop until the latter spoke. When at least he did speak, he said simply, his head bowed and his hands on his knees:

'Well, I still think that other worlds may perhaps rise higher than our reason. The mystery of heaven is unfathomable, and I for one can only bow my head.'

Then, with brow yet bent and without changing by the faintest shade in his attitude or voice, he added:

'Just hand over that sapphire cross of yours, will you? We're all alone here, and I could pull you to pieces like a straw doll.'

The utterly unaltered voice and attitude added a strange violence to that shocking change of speech. But the guarder of the relic only seemed to turn his head by the smallest section of the compass. He seemed still to have a somewhat foolish face turned to the stars. Perhaps he had not understood. Or perhaps, he had understood and sat rigid with terror.

'Yes,' said the tall priest, in the same low voice and in the same still posture, 'yes, I am Flambeau.'

Then, after a pause, he said:

'Come, will you give me that cross?'

'No,' said the other, and the monosyllable had an odd sound.

Flambeau suddenly flung off all his pontifical pretensions. The great robber leaned back in his seat and laughed low but long.

'No,' he cried; 'you won't give it to me, you proud prelate. You won't give it me, you little celibate simpleton. Shall I tell you why you won't give it me? Because I've got it already in my own breast-pocket.'

The small man from Essex turned what seemed to be a dazed face in the dusk, and said, with the timid eagerness of 'The Private Secretary':

'Are—are you sure?'

Flambeau yelled with delight.

'Really, you're as good as a three-act farce,' he cried. 'Yes, you turnip, I am quite sure. I had the sense to make a duplicate of the right parcel, and now, my friend, you've got the duplicate, and I've got the jewels. An old dodge, Father Brown—a very old dodge.'

'Yes,' said Father Brown, and passed his hand through his hair with the same strange vagueness of manner. 'Yes, I've heard of it before.'

The colossus of crime leaned over to the little rustic priest with a sort of sudden interest.

'You have heard of it?' he asked. 'Where have you heard of it?'

'Well, I mustn't tell you his name, of course,' said the little man simply. 'He was a penitent, you know. He had lived prosperously for about twenty years entirely on duplicate brown-paper parcels. And so, you see, when I began to suspect you, I thought of this poor chap's way of doing it at once.'

'Began to suspect me,' repeated the outlaw with increased intensity. 'Did you really have the gumption to suspect me just because I brought you up to this bare part of the heath?'

'No, no,' said Brown with an air of apology. 'You see, I suspected you when we first met. It's that little bulge up the sleeve where you people have the spiked bracelet.'

'How in Tartarus,' cried Flambeau, 'did you ever hear of the spiked bracelet?'

'Oh, one's little flock, you know!' said Father Brown, arching his eyebrows rather blankly. 'When I was a curate in Hartlepool, there were three of them with spiked bracelets. So, as I suspected you from the first, don't you see, I made sure that the cross should go safe, anyhow. I'm afraid I watched you, you know. So at last I saw you change the parcels. Then, don't you see, I changed them back again. And then I left the right one behind.'

'Left it behind?' repeated Flambeau, and for the first time there was another note in his voice beside his triumph.

'Well, it was like this,' said the little priest, speaking in the same unaffected way. 'I went back to that sweet shop and asked if I'd left a parcel, and gave them a particular address if it turned up. Well, I knew I hadn't; but when I went away again I did. So, instead of running after me with that valuable parcel, they have sent it flying to a friend of mine in Westminster.' Then he added rather sadly: 'I learnt that, too, from a poor fellow in Hartlepool. He used to do it with handbags he stole at railway stations, but he's in a monastery now. Oh, one gets to know, you know,' he added, rubbing his head again with the same sort of desperate apology. 'We can't help it, being priests. People come and tell us these things.'

Flambeau tore a brown-paper parcel out of his inner pocket and rent it in pieces. There was nothing but paper and sticks of lead inside it. He sprang to his feet with a gigantic gesture, and cried:

'I don't believe you. I don't believe a bumpkin like you could manage all that. I believe you've still got the stuff on you, and if you don't give it up—why, we're all alone, and I'll take it by force!'

'No,' said Father Brown simply, and stood up also; 'you won't take it by force. First, because I really haven't still got it. And second, because we are not alone.'

Flambeau stopped in his stride forward.

'Behind that tree,' said Father Brown, pointing, 'are two strong policemen and the greatest detective alive. How did they come here, do you ask? Why, I brought them, of course! How did I do it? Why, I'll tell you if you like! Lord bless you, we have to know twenty such things when we work among the criminal classes! Well, I wasn't sure you were a thief, and it would never do to make a scandal against one of our own clergy. So I just tested you to see if anything would make you show yourself. A man generally makes a small scene if he finds salt in his coffee; if he doesn't, he has some reason for keeping quiet. I changed the salt and sugar, and you kept quiet. A man generally objects if his bill is three times too big. If he pays it, he has some motive for passing unnoticed. I altered your bill, and you paid it.'

The world was waiting for Flambeau to leap up like a tiger. But he was held back as by a spell; he was stunned with the utmost curiosity.

'Well,' went on Father Brown, with lumbering lucidity, 'as you wouldn't leave any tracks for the police, of course somebody had to. At every place we went to, I took care to do something that would get us talked about for the rest of the day. I didn't do much harm—a splashed wall, spilt apples, a broken window; but I saved the cross, as the cross will always be saved. It is at Westminster by now. I rather wonder you didn't stop it with the Donkey's Whistle.'

'With the what?' asked Flambeau.

'I'm glad you've never heard of it,' said the priest, making a face. 'It's a foul thing. I'm sure you're too good a man for a Whistler. I couldn't have countered it even with the Spots myself; I'm not strong enough in the legs.'

'What on earth are you talking about?' asked the other.

'Well, I did think you'd know the Spots,' said Father Brown, agreeably surprised. 'Oh, you can't have gone so very wrong yet!'

'How in blazes do you know all these horrors?' cried

Flambeau.

The shadow of a smile crossed the round, simple face of his clerical opponent.

'Oh, by being a celibate simpleton, I suppose,' he said. 'Has it never struck you that a man who does next to nothing but hear men's real sins is not likely to be wholly unaware of human evil? But, as a matter of fact, another part of my trade, too, made me sure you weren't a priest.' 'What?' asked the thief, almost gaping. 'You attacked reason,' said Father Brown. 'It's bad theology.' And even as he turned away to collect his property, the three policemen came out from under the twilight trees. Flambeau was an artist and a sportsman. He stepped back and swept Valentin a great bow. 'Do not bow to me, mon ami,' said Valentin, with silver clearness. 'Let us both bow to our master.' And they both stood an instant uncovered, while the little Essex priest blinked about for his umbrella.

4

THE BOTTOMLESS WELL

In an oasis, or green island, in the red and yellow seas of sand that stretch beyond Europe toward the sunrise, there can be found a rather fantastic contrast, which is none the less typical of such a place, since international treaties have made it an outpost of the British occupation. The site is famous among archaeologists for something that is hardly a monument, but merely a hole in the ground. But it is a round shaft, like that of a well, and probably a part of some great irrigation works of remote and disputed date, perhaps more ancient than anything in that ancient land. There is a green fringe of palm and prickly pear round the black mouth of the well; but nothing of the upper masonry remains except two bulky and battered stones standing like the pillars of a gateway of nowhere, in which some of the more transcendental archaeologists, in certain moods at moonrise or sunset, think they can trace the faint lines of figures or features of more than Babylonian monstrosity; while the more rationalistic archaeologists, in the more rational hours of daylight, see nothing but two shapeless rocks. It may have been noticed, however, that all Englishmen are not archaeologists. Many of those assembled in such a place for official and military purposes have hobbies other than archaeology. And it is a solemn fact that the English in this Eastern exile have contrived to make a small golf links out of the green scrub and sand; with a comfortable clubhouse at one end of it and this primeval monument at the other. They did not actually use this archaic abyss as a bunker, because it was by tradition unfathomable, and even for practical purposes unfathomed. Any sporting projectile sent into it might be counted most literally as a lost ball. But they often sauntered round it in their interludes of talking and smoking cigarettes, and one of them had just come down from the clubhouse to find another gazing somewhat moodily into the well.

Both the Englishmen wore light clothes and white pith helmets and puggrees, but there, for the most part, their resemblance ended. And they both almost simultaneously said the same word, but they said it on two totally different notes of the voice.

'Have you heard the news?' asked the man from the club. 'Splendid.'

'Splendid,' replied the man by the well. But the first man pronounced the word as a young man might say it about a woman, and the second as an old man might say it about the weather, not without sincerity, but certainly without fervor.

And in this the tone of the two men was sufficiently typical of them. The first, who was a certain Captain Boyle, was of a bold and boyish type, dark, and with a sort of native heat in his face that did not belong to the atmosphere of the East, but rather to the ardors and ambitions of the West. The other was an older man and certainly an older resident, a civilian official—Horne Fisher; and his drooping eyelids and drooping light mustache expressed all the paradox of the Englishman in the East. He was much too hot to be anything but cool.

Neither of them thought it necessary to mention what it was that was splendid. That would indeed have been superfluous conversation about something that everybody knew. The striking victory over a menacing combination of Turks and Arabs in the north, won by troops under the command of Lord

Hastings, the veteran of so many striking victories, was already spread by the newspapers all over the Empire, let alone to this small garrison so near to the battlefield.

'Now, no other nation in the world could have done a thing like that,' cried Captain Boyle, emphatically.

Horne Fisher was still looking silently into the well; a moment later he answered: 'We certainly have the art of unmaking mistakes. That's where the poor old Prussians went wrong. They could only make mistakes and stick to them. There is really a certain talent in unmaking a mistake.'

'What do you mean,' asked Boyle, 'what mistakes?'

'Well, everybody knows it looked like biting off more than he could chew,' replied Horne Fisher. It was a peculiarity of Mr. Fisher that he always said that everybody knew things which about one person in two million was ever allowed to hear of. 'And it was certainly jolly lucky that Travers turned up so well in the nick of time. Odd how often the right thing's been done for us by the second in command, even when a great man was first in command. Like Colborne at Waterloo.'

'It ought to add a whole province to the Empire,' observed the other.

'Well, I suppose the Zimmernes would have insisted on it as far as the canal,' observed Fisher, thoughtfully, 'though everybody knows adding provinces doesn't always pay much nowadays.'

Captain Boyle frowned in a slightly puzzled fashion. Being cloudily conscious of never having heard of the Zimmernes in his life, he could only remark, stolidly:

'Well, one can't be a Little Englander.'

Horne Fisher smiled, and he had a pleasant smile.

'Every man out here is a Little Englander,' he said. 'He wishes he were back in Little England.'

'I don't know what you're talking about, I'm afraid,' said

the younger man, rather suspiciously. 'One would think you didn't really admire Hastings or—or—anything.'

'I admire him no end,' replied Fisher. 'He's by far the best man for this post; he understands the Moslems and can do anything with them. That's why I'm all against pushing Travers against him, merely because of this last affair.'

'I really don't understand what you're driving at,' said the other, frankly.

'Perhaps it isn't worth understanding,' answered Fisher, lightly, 'and, anyhow, we needn't talk politics. Do you know the Arab legend about that well?'

'I'm afraid I don't know much about Arab legends,' said Boyle, rather stiffly.

'That's rather a mistake,' replied Fisher, 'especially from your point of view. Lord Hastings himself is an Arab legend. That is perhaps the very greatest thing he really is. If his reputation went it would weaken us all over Asia and Africa. Well, the story about that hole in the ground, that goes down nobody knows where, has always fascinated me, rather. It's Mohammedan in form now, but I shouldn't wonder if the tale is a long way older than Mohammed. It's all about somebody they call the Sultan Aladdin, not our friend of the lamp, of course, but rather like him in having to do with genii or giants or something of that sort. They say he commanded the giants to build him a sort of pagoda, rising higher and higher above all the stars. The Utmost for the Highest, as the people said when they built the Tower of Babel. But the builders of the Tower of Babel were quite modest and domestic people, like mice, compared with old Aladdin. They only wanted a tower that would reach heaven—a mere trifle. He wanted a tower that would pass heaven and rise above it, and go on rising for ever and ever. And Allah cast him down to earth with a thunderbolt, which sank into the earth, boring a hole deeper and deeper, till it made a well that was without a bottom as the tower was to have been without a top. And down that inverted tower of darkness the soul of the proud Sultan is falling forever and ever.'

'What a queer chap you are,' said Boyle. 'You talk as if a fellow could believe those fables.'

'Perhaps I believe the moral and not the fable,' answered Fisher.

'But here comes Lady Hastings. You know her, I think.'

The clubhouse on the golf links was used, of course, for many other purposes besides that of golf. It was the only social center of the garrison beside the strictly military headquarters; it had a billiard room and a bar, and even an excellent reference library for those officers who were so perverse as to take their profession seriously. Among these was the great general himself, whose head of silver and face of bronze, like that of a brazen eagle, were often to be found bent over the charts and folios of the library. The great Lord Hastings believed in science and study, as in other severe ideals of life, and had given much paternal advice on the point to young Boyle, whose appearances in that place of research were rather more intermittent. It was from one of these snatches of study that the young man had just come out through the glass doors of the library on to the golf links. But, above all, the club was so appointed as to serve the social conveniences of ladies at least as much as gentlemen, and Lady Hastings was able to play the queen in such a society almost as much as in her own ballroom. She was eminently calculated and, as some said, eminently inclined to play such a part. She was much younger than her husband, an attractive and sometimes dangerously attractive lady; and Mr. Horne Fisher looked after her a little sardonically as she swept away with the young soldier. Then his rather dreary eye strayed to the green and prickly growths round the well, growths of that curious cactus formation in which one thick leaf grows directly out of the other without stalk or twig. It gave his fanciful mind a sinister feeling of a blind growth without shape or purpose. A flower or shrub in the West grows to the blossom which is its crown, and is content. But this was as if hands could grow out of hands or legs grow out of legs in a nightmare. 'Always adding a province to the Empire,' he said, with a smile, and then added, more sadly, 'but I doubt if I was right, after all!'

A strong but genial voice broke in on his meditations and he looked up and smiled, seeing the face of an old friend. The voice was, indeed, rather more genial than the face, which was at the first glance decidedly grim. It was a typically legal face, with angular jaws and heavy, grizzled eyebrows; and it belonged to an eminently legal character, though he was now attached in a semimilitary capacity to the police of that wild district. Cuthbert Grayne was perhaps more of a criminologist than either a lawyer or a policeman, but in his more barbarous surroundings he had proved successful in turning himself into a practical combination of all three. The discovery of a whole series of strange Oriental crimes stood to his credit. But as few people were acquainted with, or attracted to, such a hobby or branch of knowledge, his intellectual life was somewhat solitary. Among the few exceptions was Horne Fisher, who had a curious capacity for talking to almost anybody about almost anything.

'Studying botany, or is it archaeology?' inquired Grayne. 'I shall never come to the end of your interests, Fisher. I should say that what you don't know isn't worth knowing.'

'You are wrong,' replied Fisher, with a very unusual abruptness, and even bitterness. 'It's what I do know that isn't worth knowing. All the seamy side of things, all the secret reasons and rotten motives and bribery and blackmail they call politics. I needn't be so proud of having been down all these sewers that I should brag about it to the little boys in the street.'

'What do you mean? What's the matter with you?' asked his friend.

'I never knew you taken like this before.'

'I'm ashamed of myself,' replied Fisher. 'I've just been throwing cold water on the enthusiasms of a boy.'

'Even that explanation is hardly exhaustive,' observed the criminal expert.

'Damned newspaper nonsense the enthusiasms were, of course,' continued Fisher, 'but I ought to know that at that age illusions can be ideals. And they're better than the reality, anyhow. But there is one very ugly responsibility about jolting a young man out of the rut of the most rotten ideal.'

'And what may that be?' inquired his friend.

'It's very apt to set him off with the same energy in a much worse direction,' answered Fisher; 'a pretty endless sort of direction, a bottomless pit as deep as the bottomless well.'

Fisher did not see his friend until a fortnight later, when he found himself in the garden at the back of the clubhouse on the opposite side from the links, a garden heavily colored and scented with sweet semitropical plants in the glow of a desert sunset. Two other men were with him, the third being the now celebrated second in command, familiar to everybody as Tom Travers, a lean, dark man, who looked older than his years, with a furrow in his brow and something morose about the very shape of his black mustache. They had just been served with black coffee by the Arab now officiating as the temporary servant of the club, though he was a figure already familiar, and even famous, as the old servant of the general. He went by the name of Said, and was notable among other Semites for that unnatural length of his yellow face and height of his narrow forehead which is sometimes seen among them, and gave an irrational impression of something sinister, in spite of his agreeable smile.

'I never feel as if I could quite trust that fellow,' said Grayne, when the man had gone away. 'It's very unjust, I take it, for he was certainly devoted to Hastings, and saved his life, they say. But Arabs are often like that, loyal to one man. I can't help feeling he might cut anybody else's throat, and even do it treacherously.'

'Well,' said Travers, with a rather sour smile, 'so long as he leaves Hastings alone the world won't mind much.'

There was a rather embarrassing silence, full of memories of the great battle, and then Horne Fisher said, quietly:

'The newspapers aren't the world, Tom. Don't you worry about them. Everybody in your world knows the truth well enough.'

'I think we'd better not talk about the general just now,' remarked Grayne, 'for he's just coming out of the club.'

'He's not coming here,' said Fisher. 'He's only seeing his wife to the car.'

As he spoke, indeed, the lady came out on the steps of the club, followed by her husband, who then went swiftly in front of her to open the garden gate. As he did so she turned back and spoke for a moment to a solitary man still sitting in a cane chair in the shadow of the doorway, the only man left in the deserted club save for the three that lingered in the garden. Fisher peered for a moment into the shadow, and saw that it was Captain Boyle.

The next moment, rather to their surprise, the general reappeared and, remounting the steps, spoke a word or two to Boyle in his turn. Then he signaled to Said, who hurried up with two cups of coffee, and the two men re-entered the club, each carrying his cup in his hand. The next moment a gleam of white light in the growing darkness showed that the electric lamps had been turned on in the library beyond.

'Coffee and scientific researches,' said Travers, grimly. 'All the luxuries of learning and theoretical research. Well, I must be going, for I have my work to do as well.' And he got up rather stiffly, saluted his companions, and strode away into the dusk.

'I only hope Boyle is sticking to scientific researches,' said Horne Fisher. 'I'm not very comfortable about him myself. But let's talk about something else.'

They talked about something else longer than they probably imagined, until the tropical night had come and a splendid moon painted the whole scene with silver; but before it was bright enough to see by Fisher had already noted that the lights in the library had been abruptly extinguished. He waited for the two men to come out by the garden entrance, but nobody came.

'They must have gone for a stroll on the links,' he said.

'Very possibly,' replied Grayne. 'It's going to be a beautiful night.'

A moment or two after he had spoken they heard a voice hailing them out of the shadow of the clubhouse, and were astonished to perceive Travers hurrying toward them, calling out as he came:

'I shall want your help, you fellows,' he cried. 'There's something pretty bad out on the links.'

They found themselves plunging through the club smoking room and the library beyond, in complete darkness, mental as well as material. But Horne Fisher, in spite of his affectation of indifference, was a person of a curious and almost transcendental sensibility to atmospheres, and he already felt the presence of something more than an accident. He collided with a piece of furniture in the library, and almost shuddered with the shock, for the thing moved as he could never have fancied a piece of furniture moving. It seemed to move like a living thing, yielding and yet striking back. The next moment Grayne had turned on the lights, and he saw he had only stumbled against one of the revolving bookstands that had swung round and struck him; but his involuntary recoil had revealed to him his own subconscious sense of something mysterious and monstrous. There were several of these revolving bookcases standing here and there about the library; on one of them stood the two cups of coffee, and on another a large open book. It was Budge's book on Egyptian hieroglyphics, with colored plates of strange birds and gods, and even as he rushed past, he was conscious of something odd about the fact that this, and not any work of military science, should be open in that place at that moment. He was even conscious of the gap in the well-lined bookshelf from which it had been taken, and it seemed almost to gape at him in an ugly fashion, like a gap in the teeth of some sinister face.

A run brought them in a few minutes to the other side of the ground in front of the bottomless well, and a few yards from it, in a moonlight almost as broad as daylight, they saw what they had come to see.

The great Lord Hastings lay prone on his face, in a posture in which there was a touch of something strange and stiff, with one elbow erect above his body, the arm being doubled, and his big, bony hand clutching the rank and ragged grass. A few feet away was Boyle, almost as motionless, but supported on his hands and knees, and staring at the body. It might have been no more than shock and accident; but there was something ungainly and unnatural about the quadrupedal posture and the gaping face. It was as if his reason had fled from him. Behind, there was nothing but the clear blue southern sky, and the beginning of the desert, except for the two great broken stones in front of the well. And it was in such a light and atmosphere that men could fancy they traced in them enormous and evil faces, looking down.

Horne Fisher stooped and touched the strong hand that was still clutching the grass, and it was as cold as a stone. He knelt by the body and was busy for a moment applying other tests; then he rose again, and said, with a sort of confident despair:

'Lord Hastings is dead.'

There was a stony silence, and then Travers remarked, gruffly: 'This is your department, Grayne; I will leave you to question Captain Boyle. I can make no sense of what he says.'

Boyle had pulled himself together and risen to his feet, but his face still wore an awful expression, making it like a new mask or the face of another man.

'I was looking at the well,' he said, 'and when I turned he had fallen down.'

Grayne's face was very dark. 'As you say, this is my affair,' he said. 'I must first ask you to help me carry him to the library and let me examine things thoroughly.'

When they had deposited the body in the library, Grayne turned to Fisher and said, in a voice that had recovered its fullness and confidence, 'I am going to lock myself in and make a thorough examination first. I look to you to keep in touch with the others and make a preliminary examination of Boyle. I will talk to him later. And just telephone to headquarters for a policeman, and let him come here at once and stand by till I want him.'

Without more words the great criminal investigator went into the lighted library, shutting the door behind him, and Fisher, without replying, turned and began to talk quietly to Travers. 'It is curious,' he said, 'that the thing should happen just in front of that place.'

'It would certainly be very curious,' replied Travers, 'if the place played any part in it.'

'I think,' replied Fisher, 'that the part it didn't play is more curious still.'

And with these apparently meaningless words he turned to the shaken Boyle and, taking his arm, began to walk him up and down in the moonlight, talking in low tones.

Dawn had begun to break abrupt and white when Cuthbert Grayne turned out the lights in the library and came out on to the links. Fisher was lounging about alone, in his listless fashion; but the police messenger for whom he had sent was standing at attention in the background.

'I sent Boyle off with Travers,' observed Fisher, carelessly; 'he'll look after him, and he'd better have some sleep, anyhow.'

'Did you get anything out of him?' asked Grayne. 'Did he tell you what he and Hastings were doing?'

'Yes,' answered Fisher, 'he gave me a pretty clear account, after all. He said that after Lady Hastings went off in the car the general asked him to take coffee with him in the library and look up a point about local antiquities. He himself was beginning to look for Budge's book in one of the revolving bookstands when the general found it in one of the bookshelves on the wall. After looking at some of the plates they went out, it would seem, rather abruptly, on to the links, and walked toward the old well; and while Boyle was looking into it he heard a thud behind him, and turned round to find the general lying as we found him. He himself dropped on his knees to examine the body, and then was paralyzed with a sort of terror and could not come nearer to it or touch it. But I think very little of that; people caught in a real shock of surprise are sometimes found in the queerest postures.'

Grayne wore a grim smile of attention, and said, after a short silence:

'Well, he hasn't told you many lies. It's really a creditably clear and consistent account of what happened, with everything of importance left out.'

'Have you discovered anything in there?' asked Fisher.

'I have discovered everything,' answered Grayne.

Fisher maintained a somewhat gloomy silence, as the other resumed his explanation in quiet and assured tones.

'You were quite right, Fisher, when you said that young fellow was in danger of going down dark ways toward the pit. Whether or no, as you fancied, the jolt you gave to his view of the general had anything to do with it, he has not been treating the general well for some time. It's an unpleasant business, and I don't want to dwell on it; but it's pretty plain that his wife was not treating him well, either. I don't know how far it went, but it went as far as concealment, anyhow; for when Lady Hastings spoke to Boyle it was to tell him she had hidden a note in the Budge book in the library. The general overheard, or came somehow to know, and he went straight to the book and found it. He confronted Boyle with it, and they had a scene, of course. And Boyle was confronted with something else; he was confronted with an awful alternative, in which the life of one old man meant ruin and his death meant triumph and even happiness.'

'Well,' observed Fisher, at last, 'I don't blame him for not telling you the woman's part of the story. But how do you know about the letter?'

'I found it on the general's body,' answered Grayne, 'but I found worse things than that. The body had stiffened in the way rather peculiar to poisons of a certain Asiatic sort. Then I examined the coffee cups, and I knew enough chemistry to find poison in the dregs of one of them. Now, the General went straight to the bookcase, leaving his cup of coffee on the bookstand in the middle of the room. While his back was turned, and Boyle was pretending to examine the bookstand, he was left alone with the coffee cup. The poison takes about ten minutes to act, and ten minutes' walk would bring them to the bottomless well.'

'Yes,' remarked Fisher, 'and what about the bottomless well?'

'What has the bottomless well got to do with it?' asked his friend.

'It has nothing to do with it,' replied Fisher. 'That is what I find utterly confounding and incredible.'

'And why should that particular hole in the ground have anything to do with it?'

'It is a particular hole in your case,' said Fisher. 'But I won't insist on that just now. By the way, there is another thing I ought to tell you. I said I sent Boyle away in charge of Travers. It would be just as true to say I sent Travers in charge of Boyle.'

'You don't mean to say you suspect Tom Travers?' cried the other.

'He was a deal bitterer against the general than Boyle ever was,' observed Horne Fisher, with a curious indifference.

'Man, you're not saying what you mean,' cried Grayne. 'I tell you I found the poison in one of the coffee cups.'

'There was always Said, of course,' added Fisher, 'either for hatred or hire. We agreed he was capable of almost anything.'

'And we agreed he was incapable of hurting his master,' retorted Grayne.

'Well, well,' said Fisher, amiably, 'I dare say you are right; but I should just like to have a look at the library and the coffee cups.'

He passed inside, while Grayne turned to the policeman in attendance and handed him a scribbled note, to be telegraphed from headquarters. The man saluted and hurried off; and Grayne, following his friend into the library, found him beside the bookstand in the middle of the room, on which were the empty cups.

'This is where Boyle looked for Budge, or pretended to look for him, according to your account,' he said.

As Fisher spoke he bent down in a half-crouching attitude,

to look at the volumes in the low, revolving shelf, for the whole bookstand was not much higher than an ordinary table. The next moment he sprang up as if he had been stung.

'Oh, my God!' he cried.

Very few people, if any, had ever seen Mr. Horne Fisher behave as he behaved just then. He flashed a glance at the door, saw that the open window was nearer, went out of it with a flying leap, as if over a hurdle, and went racing across the turf, in the track of the disappearing policeman. Grayne, who stood staring after him, soon saw his tall, loose figure, returning, restored to all its normal limpness and air of leisure. He was fanning himself slowly with a piece of paper, the telegram he had so violently intercepted.

'Lucky I stopped that,' he observed. 'We must keep this affair as quiet as death. Hastings must die of apoplexy or heart disease.'

'What on earth is the trouble?' demanded the other investigator.

'The trouble is,' said Fisher, 'that in a few days we should have had a very agreeable alternative—of hanging an innocent man or knocking the British Empire to hell.'

'Do you mean to say,' asked Grayne, 'that this infernal crime is not to be punished?'

Fisher looked at him steadily. 'It is already punished,' he said.

After a moment's pause he went on. 'You reconstructed the crime with admirable skill, old chap, and nearly all you said was true. Two men with two coffee cups did go into the library and did put their cups on the bookstand and did go together to the well, and one of them was a murderer and had put poison in the other's cup. But it was not done while Boyle was looking at the revolving bookcase. He did look at it, though, searching for the Budge book with the note in it, but I fancy that Hastings had already moved it to the shelves on the wall. It was part of that grim game that he should find it first.

'Now, how does a man search a revolving bookcase? He does not generally hop all round it in a squatting attitude, like a frog. He simply gives it a touch and makes it revolve.'

He was frowning at the floor as he spoke, and there was a light under his heavy lids that was not often seen there. The mysticism that was buried deep under all the cynicism of his experience was awake and moving in the depths. His voice took unexpected turns and inflections, almost as if two men were speaking.

'That was what Boyle did; he barely touched the thing, and it went round as easily as the world goes round. Yes, very much as the world goes round, for the hand that turned it was not his. God, who turns the wheel of all the stars, touched that wheel and brought it full circle, that His dreadful justice might return.'

'I am beginning,' said Grayne, slowly, 'to have some hazy and horrible idea of what you mean.'

'It is very simple,' said Fisher, 'when Boyle straightened himself from his stooping posture, something had happened which he had not noticed, which his enemy had not noticed, which nobody had noticed. The two coffee cups had exactly changed places.'

The rocky face of Grayne seemed to have sustained a shock in silence; not a line of it altered, but his voice when it came was unexpectedly weakened.

'I see what you mean,' he said, 'and, as you say, the less said about it the better. It was not the lover who tried to get rid of the husband, but—the other thing. And a tale like that about a man like that would ruin us here. Had you any guess of this at the start?'

'The bottomless well, as I told you,' answered Fisher, quietly, 'that was what stumped me from the start. Not because it had anything to do with it, because it had nothing to do with it.'

He paused a moment, as if choosing an approach, and then went on: 'When a man knows his enemy will be dead in ten minutes, and takes him to the edge of an unfathomable pit, he means to throw his body into it. What else should he do? A born fool would have the sense to do it, and Boyle is not a born fool. Well, why did not Boyle do it? The more I thought of it the more I suspected there was some mistake in the murder, so to speak. Somebody had taken somebody there to throw him in, and yet he was not thrown in. I had already an ugly, unformed idea of some substitution or reversal of parts; then I stooped to turn the bookstand myself, by accident, and I instantly knew everything, for I saw the two cups revolve once more, like moons in the sky.'

After a pause, Cuthbert Grayne said, 'And what are we to say to the newspapers?'

'My friend, Harold March, is coming along from Cairo today,' said Fisher. 'He is a very brilliant and successful journalist. But for all that he's a thoroughly honorable man, so you must not tell him the truth.'

Half an hour later Fisher was again walking to and fro in front of the clubhouse, with Captain Boyle, the latter by this time with a very buffeted and bewildered air; perhaps a sadder and a wiser man.

'What about me, then?' he was saying. 'Am I cleared? Am I not going to be cleared?'

'I believe and hope,' answered Fisher, 'that you are not going to be suspected. But you are certainly not going to be cleared. There must be no suspicion against him, and therefore no suspicion against you. Any suspicion against him, let alone such a story against him, would knock us endways from Malta to Mandalay. He was a hero as well as a holy terror among the Moslems. Indeed, you might almost call him a Moslem hero in the English service. Of course he got on with them partly because of his own little dose of Eastern blood; he got it from his mother, the dancer from Damascus; everybody knows that.'

'Oh,' repeated Boyle, mechanically, staring at him with round eyes, 'everybody knows that.'

'I dare say there was a touch of it in his jealousy and ferocious vengeance,' went on Fisher. 'But, for all that, the crime would ruin us among the Arabs, all the more because it was something like a crime against hospitality. It's been hateful for you and it's pretty horrid for me. But there are some things that damned well can't be done, and while I'm alive that's one of them.'

'What do you mean?' asked Boyle, glancing at him curiously.

'Why should you, of all people, be so passionate about it?'

Horne Fisher looked at the young man with a baffling expression.

'I suppose,' he said, 'it's because I'm a Little Englander.'

'I can never make out what you mean by that sort of thing,' answered Boyle, doubtfully.

'Do you think England is so little as all that?' said Fisher, with a warmth in his cold voice, 'that it can't hold a man across a few thousand miles. You lectured me with a lot of ideal patriotism, my young friend; but it's practical patriotism now for you and me, and with no lies to help it. You talked as if everything always went right with us all over the world, in a triumphant crescendo culminating in Hastings. I tell you everything has gone wrong with us here, except Hastings. He was the one name we had left to conjure with, and that mustn't go as well, no, by God! It's bad enough that a gang of infernal Jews should plant us here, where there's no earthly English interest to serve, and all hell beating up against us, simply because Nosey Zimmern has lent money to half the Cabinet. It's bad enough that an old pawnbroker from Bagdad should make us fight his battles; we can't fight with our right hand cut off. Our one score was Hastings and his victory, which was really somebody else's victory. Tom Travers has to suffer, and so have you.'

Then, after a moment's silence, he pointed toward the bottomless well and said, in a quieter tone: 'I told you that I didn't believe in the philosophy of the Tower of Aladdin. I don't believe in the Empire growing until it reaches the sky; I don't believe in the Union Jack going up and up eternally like the Tower. But if you think I am going to let the Union Jack go down and down eternally, like the bottomless well, down into the blackness of the bottomless pit, down in defeat and derision, amid the jeers of the very Jews who have sucked us dry—no I won't, and that's flat; not if the Chancellor were blackmailed by twenty millionaires with their gutter rags, not if the Prime Minister married twenty Yankee Jewesses, not if Woodville and Carstairs had shares in twenty swindling mines. If the thing is really tottering, God help it, it mustn't be we who tip it over.'

Boyle was regarding him with a bewilderment that was almost fear, and had even a touch of distaste.

'Somehow,' he said, 'there seems to be something rather horrid about the things you know.'

'There is,' replied Horne Fisher. 'I am not at all pleased with my small stock of knowledge and reflection. But as it is partly responsible for your not being hanged, I don't know that you need complain of it.'

And, as if a little ashamed of his first boast, he turned and strolled away toward the bottomless well.

5

THE DUEL OF DR HIRSCH

M. Maurice Brun and M. Armand Armagnac were crossing the sunlit Champs Elysee with a kind of vivacious respectability. They were both short, brisk and bold. They both had black beards that did not seem to belong to their faces, after the strange French fashion which makes real hair look like artificial. M. Brun had a dark wedge of beard apparently affixed under his lower lip. M. Armagnac, by way of a change, had two beards; one sticking out from each corner of his emphatic chin. They were both young. They were both atheists, with a depressing fixity of outlook but great mobility of exposition. They were both pupils of the great Dr Hirsch, scientist, publicist and moralist.

M. Brun had become prominent by his proposal that the common expression 'Adieu' should be obliterated from all the French classics, and a slight fine imposed for its use in private life. 'Then,' he said, 'the very name of your imagined God will have echoed for the last time in the ear of man.' M. Armagnac specialized rather in a resistance to militarism, and wished the chorus of the Marseillaise altered from 'Aux armes, citoyens' to 'Aux greves, citoyens'. But his antimilitarism was of a peculiar and Gallic sort. An eminent and very wealthy English Quaker, who had come to see him to arrange for the disarmament of the whole planet, was rather distressed by Armagnac's proposal that (by way of beginning) the soldiers should shoot their officers.

And indeed it was in this regard that the two men differed most from their leader and father in philosophy. Dr Hirsch, though born in France and covered with the most triumphant favours of French education, was temperamentally of another type—mild, dreamy, humane; and, despite his sceptical system, not devoid of transcendentalism. He was, in short, more like a German than a Frenchman; and much as they admired him, something in the subconsciousness of these Gauls was irritated at his pleading for peace in so peaceful a manner. To their party throughout Europe, however, Paul Hirsch was a saint of science. His large and daring cosmic theories advertised his austere life and innocent, if somewhat frigid, morality; he held something of the position of Darwin doubled with the position of Tolstoy. But he was neither an anarchist nor an antipatriot; his views on disarmament were moderate and evolutionary— the Republican Government put considerable confidence in him as to various chemical improvements. He had lately even discovered a noiseless explosive, the secret of which the Government was carefully guarding.

His house stood in a handsome street near the Elysee— a street which in that strong summer seemed almost as full of foliage as the park itself; a row of chestnuts shattered the sunshine, interrupted only in one place where a large cafe ran out into the street. Almost opposite to this were the white and green blinds of the great scientist's house, an iron balcony, also painted green, running along in front of the first-floor windows. Beneath this was the entrance into a kind of court, gay with shrubs and tiles, into which the two Frenchmen passed in animated talk.

The door was opened to them by the doctor's old servant, Simon, who might very well have passed for a doctor himself, having a strict suit of black, spectacles, grey hair, and a confidential manner. In fact, he was a far more presentable man of science than his master, Dr Hirsch, who was a forked radish of a fellow, with just enough bulb of a head to make his body insignificant. With all the gravity of a great physician handling a prescription, Simon handed a letter to M. Armagnac. That gentleman ripped it up with a racial impatience, and rapidly read the following:

'I cannot come down to speak to you. There is a man in this house whom I refuse to meet. He is a Chauvinist officer, Dubosc. He is sitting on the stairs. He has been kicking the furniture about in all the other rooms; I have locked myself in my study, opposite that cafe. If you love me, go over to the cafe and wait at one of the tables outside. I will try to send him over to you. I want you to answer him and deal with him. I cannot meet him myself. I cannot: I will not.

There is going to be another Dreyfus case.

P. HIRSCH'

M. Armagnac looked at M. Brun. M. Brun borrowed the letter, read it, and looked at M. Armagnac. Then both betook themselves briskly to one of the little tables under the chestnuts opposite, where they procured two tall glasses of horrible green absinthe, which they could drink apparently in any weather and at any time. Otherwise the cafe seemed empty, except for one soldier drinking coffee at one table, and at another a large man drinking a small syrup and a priest drinking nothing.

Maurice Brun cleared his throat and said: 'Of course we must help the master in every way, but—'

There was an abrupt silence, and Armagnac said: 'He may have excellent reasons for not meeting the man himself, but—'

Before either could complete a sentence, it was evident that the invader had been expelled from the house opposite. The shrubs under the archway swayed and burst apart, as that unwelcome guest was shot out of them like a cannon-ball.

He was a sturdy figure in a small and tilted Tyrolean felt

hat, a figure that had indeed something generally Tyrolean about it. The man's shoulders were big and broad, but his legs were neat and active in knee-breeches and knitted stockings. His face was brown like a nut; he had very bright and restless brown eyes; his dark hair was brushed back stiffly in front and cropped close behind, outlining a square and powerful skull; and he had a huge black moustache like the horns of a bison. Such a substantial head is generally based on a bull neck; but this was hidden by a big coloured scarf, swathed round up the man's ears and falling in front inside his jacket like a sort of fancy waistcoat. It was a scarf of strong dead colours, dark red and old gold and purple, probably of Oriental fabrication. Altogether the man had something a shade barbaric about him; more like a Hungarian squire than an ordinary French officer. His French, however, was obviously that of a native; and his French patriotism was so impulsive as to be slightly absurd. His first act when he burst out of the archway was to call in a clarion voice down the street: 'Are there any Frenchmen here?' as if he were calling for Christians in Mecca.

Armagnac and Brun instantly stood up; but they were too late. Men were already running from the street corners; there was a small but ever-clustering crowd. With the prompt French instinct for the politics of the street, the man with the black moustache had already run across to a corner of the cafe, sprung on one of the tables, and seizing a branch of chestnut to steady himself, shouted as Camille Desmoulins once shouted when he scattered the oak-leaves among the populace.

'Frenchmen!' he volleyed; 'I cannot speak! God help me, that is why I am speaking! The fellows in their filthy parliaments who learn to speak also learn to be silent—silent as that spy cowering in the house opposite! Silent as he is when I beat on his bedroom door! Silent as he is now, though he hears my voice across this street and shakes where he sits! Oh, they can be silent eloquently— the politicians! But the time has come when we that cannot speak must speak. You are betrayed to the Prussians. Betrayed at this moment. Betrayed by that man. I am Jules Dubosc, Colonel of Artillery, Belfort. We caught a German spy in the Vosges yesterday, and a paper was found on him—a paper I hold in my hand. Oh, they tried to hush it up; but I took it direct to the man who wrote it—the man in that house! It is in his hand. It is signed with his initials. It is a direction for finding the secret of this new Noiseless Powder. Hirsch invented it; Hirsch wrote this note about it. This note is in German, and was found in a German's pocket. "Tell the man the formula for powder is in grey envelope in first drawer to the left of Secretary's desk, War Office, in red ink. He must be careful. P. H."'

He rattled short sentences like a quick-firing gun, but he was plainly the sort of man who is either mad or right. The mass of the crowd was Nationalist, and already in threatening uproar; and a minority of equally angry Intellectuals, led by Armagnac and Brun, only made the majority more militant.

'If this is a military secret,' shouted Brun, 'why do you yell about it in the street?'

'I will tell you why I do!' roared Dubosc above the roaring crowd. 'I went to this man in straight and civil style. If he had any explanation it could have been given in complete confidence. He refuses to explain. He refers me to two strangers in a cafe as to two flunkeys. He has thrown me out of the house, but I am going back into it, with the people of Paris behind me!'

A shout seemed to shake the very facade of mansions and two stones flew, one breaking a window above the balcony. The indignant Colonel plunged once more under the archway and was heard crying and thundering inside. Every instant the human sea grew wider and wider; it surged up against the rails and steps of the traitor's house; it was already certain that the place would be burst into like the Bastille, when the broken french window opened and Dr Hirsch came out on the balcony. For an instant the fury half turned to laughter; for he was an absurd figure in such a scene. His long bare neck and sloping shoulders were the shape of a champagne bottle, but that was the only festive thing about him. His coat hung on him as on a peg; he wore his carrot-coloured hair long and weedy; his cheeks and chin were fully fringed with one of those irritating beards that begin far from the mouth. He was very pale, and he wore blue spectacles.

Livid as he was, he spoke with a sort of prim decision, so that the mob fell silent in the middle of his third sentence.

'...only two things to say to you now. The first is to my foes, the second to my friends. To my foes I say: It is true I will not meet M. Dubosc, though he is storming outside this very room. It is true I have asked two other men to confront him for me. And I will tell you why! Because I will not and must not see him— because it would be against all rules of dignity and honour to see him. Before I am triumphantly cleared before a court, there is another arbitration this gentleman owes me as a gentleman, and in referring him to my seconds I am strictly—'

Armagnac and Brun were waving their hats wildly, and even the Doctor's enemies roared applause at this unexpected defiance. Once more a few sentences were inaudible, but they could hear him say: 'To my friends—I myself should always prefer weapons purely intellectual, and to these an evolved humanity will certainly confine itself. But our own most precious truth is the fundamental force of matter and heredity. My books are successful; my theories are unrefuted; but I suffer in politics from a prejudice almost physical in the French. I cannot speak like Clemenceau and Deroulede, for their words are like echoes of their pistols. The French ask for a duellist as the English ask for a sportsman. Well, I give my proofs: I will pay this barbaric bribe, and then go back to reason for the rest of my life.'

Two men were instantly found in the crowd itself to offer their services to Colonel Dubosc, who came out presently, satisfied. One was the common soldier with the coffee, who said simply: 'I will act for you, sir. I am the Duc de Valognes.' The other was the big man, whom his friend the priest sought at first to dissuade; and then walked away alone.

In the early evening a light dinner was spread at the back of the Cafe Charlemagne. Though unroofed by any glass or gilt plaster, the guests were nearly all under a delicate and irregular roof of leaves; for the ornamental trees stood so thick around and among the tables as to give something of the dimness and the dazzle of a small orchard. At one of the central tables a very stumpy little priest sat in complete solitude, and applied himself to a pile of whitebait with the gravest sort of enjoyment. His daily living being very plain, he had a peculiar taste for sudden and isolated luxuries; he was an abstemious epicure. He did not lift his eyes from his plate, round which red pepper, lemons, brown bread and butter, etc., were rigidly ranked, until a tall shadow fell across the table, and his friend Flambeau sat down opposite. Flambeau was gloomy.

'I'm afraid I must chuck this business,' said he heavily. 'I'm all on the side of the French soldiers like Dubosc, and I'm all against the French atheists like Hirsch; but it seems to me in this case we've made a mistake. The Duke and I thought it as well to investigate the charge, and I must say I'm glad we did.'

'Is the paper a forgery, then?' asked the priest

'That's just the odd thing,' replied Flambeau. 'It's exactly like Hirsch's writing, and nobody can point out any mistake in it. But it wasn't written by Hirsch. If he's a French patriot he didn't write it, because it gives information to Germany. And if he's a German spy he didn't write it, well—because it doesn't give information to Germany.'

'You mean the information is wrong?' asked Father Brown.

'Wrong,' replied the other, 'and wrong exactly where Dr Hirsch would have been right—about the hiding-place of his own secret formula in his own official department. By favour of Hirsch and the authorities, the Duke and I have actually been allowed to inspect the secret drawer at the War Office where the Hirsch formula is kept. We are the only people who have ever known it, except the inventor himself and the Minister for War; but the Minister permitted it to save Hirsch from fighting. After that we really can't support Dubosc if his revelation is a mare's nest.'

'And it is?' asked Father Brown.

'It is,' said his friend gloomily. 'It is a clumsy forgery by somebody who knew nothing of the real hiding-place. It says the paper is in the cupboard on the right of the Secretary's desk. As a fact the cupboard with the secret drawer is some way to the left of the desk. It says the grey envelope contains a long document written in red ink. It isn't written in red ink, but in ordinary black ink. It's manifestly absurd to say that Hirsch can have made a mistake about a paper that nobody knew of but himself; or can have tried to help a foreign thief by telling him to fumble in the wrong drawer. I think we must chuck it up and apologize to old Carrots.'

Father Brown seemed to cogitate; he lifted a little whitebait on his fork. 'You are sure the grey envelope was in the left cupboard?' he asked.

'Positive,' replied Flambeau. 'The grey envelope— it was a white envelope really—was—'

Father Brown put down the small silver fish and the fork and stared across at his companion. 'What?' he asked, in an altered voice.

'Well, what?' repeated Flambeau, eating heartily.

'It was not grey,' said the priest. 'Flambeau, you frighten me.'

'What the deuce are you frightened of?'

'I'm frightened of a white envelope,' said the other seriously, 'If it had only just been grey! Hang it all, it might as well have been grey. But if it was white, the whole business is black. The Doctor has been dabbling in some of the old brimstone after all.'

'But I tell you he couldn't have written such a note!' cried Flambeau. 'The note is utterly wrong about the facts. And innocent or guilty, Dr Hirsch knew all about the facts.'

'The man who wrote that note knew all about the facts,' said his clerical companion soberly. 'He could never have got 'em so wrong without knowing about 'em. You have to know an awful lot to be wrong on every subject—like the devil.'

'Do you mean—?'

'I mean a man telling lies on chance would have told some of the truth,' said his friend firmly. 'Suppose someone sent you to find a house with a green door and a blue blind, with a front garden but no back garden, with a dog but no cat, and where they drank coffee but not tea. You would say if you found no such house that it was all made up. But I say no. I say if you found a house where the door was blue and the blind green, where there was a back garden and no front garden, where cats were common and dogs instantly shot, where tea was drunk in quarts and coffee forbidden—then you would know you had found the house. The man must have known that particular house to be so accurately inaccurate.'

'But what could it mean?' demanded the diner opposite.

'I can't conceive,' said Brown; 'I don't understand this Hirsch affair at all. As long as it was only the left drawer instead of the right, and red ink instead of black, I thought it must be the chance blunders of a forger, as you say. But three is a mystical number; it finishes things. It finishes this. That the direction about the drawer, the colour of ink, the colour of envelope, should none of them be right by accident, that can't be a coincidence. It wasn't.'

'What was it, then? Treason?' asked Flambeau, resuming his dinner.

'I don't know that either,' answered Brown, with a face of blank bewilderment. 'The only thing I can think of.... Well, I never understood that Dreyfus case. I can always grasp moral evidence easier than the other sorts. I go by a man's eyes and voice, don't you know, and whether his family seems happy, and by what subjects he chooses—and avoids. Well, I was puzzled in the Dreyfus case. Not by the horrible things imputed both ways; I know (though it's not modern to say so) that human nature in the highest places is still capable of being Cenci or Borgia. No—, what puzzled me was the sincerity of both parties. I don't mean the political parties; the rank and file are always roughly honest, and often duped. I mean the persons of the play. I mean the conspirators, if they were conspirators. I mean the traitor, if he was a traitor. I mean the men who must have known the truth. Now Dreyfus went on like a man who knew he was a wronged man. And yet the French statesmen and soldiers went on as if they knew he wasn't a wronged man but simply a wrong 'un. I don't mean they behaved well; I mean they behaved as if they were sure. I can't describe these things; I know what I mean.'

'I wish I did,' said his friend. 'And what has it to do with old Hirsch?'

'Suppose a person in a position of trust,' went on the priest, 'began to give the enemy information because it was false information. Suppose he even thought he was saving his country by misleading the foreigner. Suppose this brought him into spy circles, and little loans were made to him, and little ties tied on to him. Suppose he kept up his contradictory position in a confused way by never telling the foreign spies the truth, but letting it more and more be guessed. The better part of him (what was left of it) would still say: "I have not helped the enemy; I said it was the left drawer." The meaner part of him would already be saying: "But they may have the sense to see that means the right." I think it is psychologically possible—in an enlightened age, you know.'

'It may be psychologically possible,' answered Flambeau, 'and it certainly would explain Dreyfus being certain he was wronged and his judges being sure he was guilty. But it won't wash historically, because Dreyfus's document (if it was his document) was literally correct.'

'I wasn't thinking of Dreyfus,' said Father Brown.

Silence had sunk around them with the emptying of the tables; it was already late, though the sunlight still clung to everything, as if accidentally entangled in the trees. In the stillness Flambeau shifted his seat sharply—making an isolated and echoing noise— and threw his elbow over the angle of it. 'Well,' he said, rather harshly, 'if Hirsch is not better than a timid treason-monger...'

'You mustn't be too hard on them,' said Father Brown gently. 'It's not entirely their fault; but they have no instincts. I mean those things that make a woman refuse to dance with a man or a man to touch an investment. They've been taught that it's all a matter of degree.'

'Anyhow,' cried Flambeau impatiently, 'he's not a patch on my principal; and I shall go through with it. Old Dubosc may be a bit mad, but he's a sort of patriot after all.'

Father Brown continued to consume whitebait.

Something in the stolid way he did so caused Flambeau's fierce black eyes to ramble over his companion afresh. 'What's the matter with you?' Flambeau demanded. 'Dubosc's all right in that way. You don't doubt him?'

'My friend,' said the small priest, laying down his knife and fork in a kind of cold despair, 'I doubt everything. Everything, I mean, that has happened today. I doubt the whole story, though it has been acted before my face. I doubt every sight that my eyes have seen since morning. There is something in this business quite different from the ordinary police mystery where one man is more or less lying and the other man more or less telling the truth. Here both men.... Well! I've told you the only theory I can think of that could satisfy anybody. It doesn't satisfy me.'

'Nor me either,' replied Flambeau frowning, while the other went on eating fish with an air of entire resignation. 'If all you can suggest is that notion of a message conveyed by contraries, I call it uncommonly clever, but...well, what would you call it?'

'I should call it thin,' said the priest promptly. 'I should call it uncommonly thin. But that's the queer thing about the whole business. The lie is like a schoolboy's. There are only three versions, Dubosc's and Hirsch's and that fancy of mine. Either that note was written by a French officer to ruin a French official; or it was written by the French official to help German officers; or it was written by the French official to mislead German officers. Very well. You'd expect a secret paper passing between such people, officials or officers, to look quite different from that. You'd expect, probably a cipher, certainly abbreviations; most certainly scientific and strictly professional terms. But this thing's elaborately simple, like a penny dreadful: "In the purple grotto you will find the golden casket." It looks as if... as if it were meant to be seen through at once.'

Almost before they could take it in a short figure in French uniform had walked up to their table like the wind, and sat down with a sort of thump.

'I have extraordinary news,' said the Duc de Valognes. 'I

have just come from this Colonel of ours. He is packing up to leave the country, and he asks us to make his excuses sur le terrain.'

'What?' cried Flambeau, with an incredulity quite frightful—'apologize?'

'Yes,' said the Duke gruffly; 'then and there—before everybody— when the swords are drawn. And you and I have to do it while he is leaving the country.'

'But what can this mean?' cried Flambeau. 'He can't be afraid of that little Hirsch! Confound it!' he cried, in a kind of rational rage; 'nobody could be afraid of Hirsch!'

'I believe it's some plot!' snapped Valognes—'some plot of the Jews and Freemasons. It's meant to work up glory for Hirsch...'

The face of Father Brown was commonplace, but curiously contented; it could shine with ignorance as well as with knowledge. But there was always one flash when the foolish mask fell, and the wise mask fitted itself in its place; and Flambeau, who knew his friend, knew that his friend had suddenly understood. Brown said nothing, but finished his plate of fish.

'Where did you last see our precious Colonel?' asked Flambeau, irritably.

'He's round at the Hotel Saint Louis by the Elysee, where we drove with him. He's packing up, I tell you.'

'Will he be there still, do you think?' asked Flambeau, frowning at the table.

'I don't think he can get away yet,' replied the Duke; 'he's packing to go a long journey...'

'No,' said Father Brown, quite simply, but suddenly standing up, 'for a very short journey. For one of the shortest, in fact. But we may still be in time to catch him if we go there in a motor-cab.'

Nothing more could be got out of him until the cab swept round the corner by the Hotel Saint Louis, where they got out, and he led the party up a side lane already in deep shadow with the growing dusk. Once, when the Duke impatiently asked whether Hirsch was guilty of treason or not, he answered rather absently: 'No; only of ambition—like Caesar.' Then he somewhat inconsequently added: 'He lives a very lonely life; he has had to do everything for himself.'

'Well, if he's ambitious, he ought to be satisfied now,' said Flambeau rather bitterly. 'All Paris will cheer him now our cursed Colonel has turned tail.'

'Don't talk so loud,' said Father Brown, lowering his voice, 'your cursed Colonel is just in front.'

The other two started and shrank farther back into the shadow of the wall, for the sturdy figure of their runaway principal could indeed be seen shuffling along in the twilight in front, a bag in each hand. He looked much the same as when they first saw him, except that he had changed his picturesque mountaineering knickers for a conventional pair of trousers. It was clear he was already escaping from the hotel.

The lane down which they followed him was one of those that seem to be at the back of things, and look like the wrong side of the stage scenery. A colourless, continuous wall ran down one flank of it, interrupted at intervals by dull-hued and dirt-stained doors, all shut fast and featureless save for the chalk scribbles of some passing gamin. The tops of trees, mostly rather depressing evergreens, showed at intervals over the top of the wall, and beyond them in the grey and purple gloaming could be seen the back of some long terrace of tall Parisian houses, really comparatively close, but somehow looking as inaccessible as a range of marble mountains. On the other side of the lane ran the high gilt railings of a gloomy park.

Flambeau was looking round him in rather a weird way.

'Do you know,' he said, 'there is something about this place that—'

'Hullo!' called out the Duke sharply; 'that fellow's disappeared. Vanished, like a blasted fairy!'

'He has a key,' explained their clerical friend. 'He's only gone into one of these garden doors,' and as he spoke they heard one of the dull wooden doors close again with a click in front of them.

Flambeau strode up to the door thus shut almost in his face, and stood in front of it for a moment, biting his black moustache in a fury of curiosity. Then he threw up his long arms and swung himself aloft like a monkey and stood on the top of the wall, his enormous figure dark against the purple sky, like the dark tree-tops.

The Duke looked at the priest. 'Dubosc's escape is more elaborate than we thought,' he said; 'but I suppose he is escaping from France.'

'He is escaping from everywhere,' answered Father Brown.

Valognes's eyes brightened, but his voice sank. 'Do you mean suicide?' he asked.

'You will not find his body,' replied the other.

A kind of cry came from Flambeau on the wall above. 'My God,' he exclaimed in French, 'I know what this place is now! Why, it's the back of the street where old Hirsch lives. I thought I could recognize the back of a house as well as the back of a man.'

'And Dubosc's gone in there!' cried the Duke, smiting his hip. 'Why, they'll meet after all!' And with sudden Gallic vivacity he hopped up on the wall beside Flambeau and sat there positively kicking his legs with excitement. The priest alone remained below, leaning against the wall, with his back to the whole theatre of events, and looking wistfully across to the park palings and the twinkling, twilit trees.

The Duke, however stimulated, had the instincts of an aristocrat, and desired rather to stare at the house than to spy on it; but Flambeau, who had the instincts of a burglar (and a detective), had already swung himself from the wall into the fork of a straggling tree from which he could crawl quite close to the only illuminated window in the back of the high dark house. A red blind had been pulled down over the light, but pulled crookedly, so that it gaped on one side, and by risking his neck along a branch that looked as treacherous as a twig, Flambeau could just see Colonel Dubosc walking about in a brilliantly-lighted and luxurious bedroom. But close as Flambeau was to the house, he heard the words of his colleagues by the wall, and repeated them in a low voice.

'Yes, they will meet now after all!'

'They will never meet,' said Father Brown. 'Hirsch was right when he said that in such an affair the principals must not meet. Have you read a queer psychological story by Henry James, of two persons who so perpetually missed meeting each other by accident that they began to feel quite frightened of each other, and to think it was fate? This is something of the kind, but more curious.'

'There are people in Paris who will cure them of such morbid fancies,' said Valognes vindictively. 'They will jolly well have to meet if we capture them and force them to fight.'

'They will not meet on the Day of Judgement,' said the priest. 'If God Almighty held the truncheon of the lists, if St Michael blew the trumpet for the swords to cross—even then, if one of them stood ready, the other would not come.'

'Oh, what does all this mysticism mean?' cried the Duc de Valognes, impatiently; 'why on earth shouldn't they meet like other people?'

'They are the opposite of each other,' said Father Brown, with a queer kind of smile. 'They contradict each other. They cancel out, so to speak.'

He continued to gaze at the darkening trees opposite, but Valognes turned his head sharply at a suppressed exclamation from Flambeau. That investigator, peering into the lighted room, had just seen the Colonel, after a pace or two, proceed to take his coat off. Flambeau's first thought was that this really looked like a fight; but he soon dropped the thought for another. The solidity and squareness of Dubosc's chest and shoulders was all a powerful piece of padding and came off with his coat. In his shirt and trousers he was a comparatively slim gentleman, who walked across the bedroom to the bathroom with no more pugnacious purpose than that of washing himself. He bent over a basin, dried his dripping hands and face on a towel, and turned again so that the strong light fell on his face. His brown complexion had gone, his big black moustache had gone; he—was clean-shaven and very pale. Nothing remained of the Colonel but his bright, hawk-like, brown eyes. Under the wall Father Brown was going on in heavy meditation, as if to himself.

'It is all just like what I was saying to Flambeau. These opposites won't do. They don't work. They don't fight. If it's white instead of black, and solid instead of liquid, and so on all along the line—then there's something wrong, Monsieur, there's something wrong. One of these men is fair and the other dark, one stout and the other slim, one strong and the other weak. One has a moustache and no beard, so you can't see his mouth; the other has a beard and no moustache, so you can't see his chin. One has hair cropped to his skull, but a scarf to hide his neck; the other has low shirt-collars, but long hair to hide his skull. It's all too neat and correct, Monsieur, and there's something wrong. Things made so opposite are things that cannot quarrel. Wherever the one sticks out the other sinks in. Like a face and a mask, like a lock and a key...'

Flambeau was peering into the house with a visage as white as a sheet. The occupant of the room was standing with his back to him, but in front of a looking-glass, and had already fitted round his face a sort of framework of rank red hair, hanging disordered from the head and clinging round the jaws and chin while leaving the mocking mouth uncovered. Seen thus in the glass the white face looked like the face of Judas laughing horribly and surrounded by capering flames of hell. For a spasm Flambeau saw the fierce, red-brown eyes dancing, then they were covered with a pair of blue spectacles. Slipping on a loose black coat, the figure vanished towards the front of the house. A few moments later a roar of popular applause from the street beyond announced that Dr Hirsch had once more appeared upon the balcony.

6

THE SECRET GARDEN

Aristide Valentin, Chief of the Paris Police, was late for his dinner, and some of his guests began to arrive before him. These were, however, reassured by his confidential servant, Ivan, the old man with a scar, and a face almost as grey as his moustaches, who always sat at a table in the entrance hall—a hall hung with weapons. Valentin's house was perhaps as peculiar and celebrated as its master. It was an old house, with high walls and tall poplars almost overhanging the Seine; but the oddity—and perhaps the police value—of its architecture was this: that there was no ultimate exit at all except through this front door, which was guarded by Ivan and the armoury. The garden was large and elaborate, and there were many exits from the house into the garden. But there was no exit from the garden into the world outside; all round it ran a tall, smooth, unscalable wall with special spikes at the top; no bad garden, perhaps, for a man to reflect in whom some hundred criminals had sworn to kill.

As Ivan explained to the guests, their host had telephoned that he was detained for ten minutes. He was, in truth, making some last arrangements about executions and such ugly things; and though these duties were rootedly repulsive to him, he always performed them with precision. Ruthless in the pursuit of criminals, he was very mild about their punishment. Since he had been supreme over French—and largely over European—policial methods, his great influence had been honourably used for the mitigation of sentences and the purification of prisons.

He was one of the great humanitarian French freethinkers; and the only thing wrong with them is that they make mercy even colder than justice.

When Valentin arrived he was already dressed in black clothes and the red rosette—an elegant figure, his dark beard already streaked with grey. He went straight through his house to his study, which opened on the grounds behind. The garden door of it was open, and after he had carefully locked his box in its official place, he stood for a few seconds at the open door looking out upon the garden. A sharp moon was fighting with the flying rags and tatters of a storm, and Valentin regarded it with a wistfulness unusual in such scientific natures as his. Perhaps such scientific natures have some psychic prevision of the most tremendous problem of their lives. From any such occult mood, at least, he quickly recovered, for he knew he was late, and that his guests had already begun to arrive. A glance at his drawing-room when he entered it was enough to make certain that his principal guest was not there, at any rate. He saw all the other pillars of the little party; he saw Lord Galloway, the English Ambassador—a choleric old man with a russet face like an apple, wearing the blue ribbon of the Garter. He saw Lady Galloway, slim and threadlike, with silver hair and a face sensitive and superior. He saw her daughter, Lady Margaret Graham, a pale and pretty girl with an elfish face and copper-coloured hair. He saw the Duchess of Mont St. Michel, black-eyed and opulent, and with her her two daughters, black-eyed and opulent also. He saw Dr. Simon, a typical French scientist, with glasses, a pointed brown beard, and a forehead barred with those parallel wrinkles which are the penalty of superciliousness, since they come through constantly elevating the eyebrows. He saw Father Brown, of Cobhole, in Essex, whom he had recently met in England. He saw—perhaps with more interest than any of these—a tall man in uniform, who had bowed to the Galloways without receiving any very hearty acknowledgment, and who now advanced alone to pay his respects to his host. This was Commandant O'Brien, of the French Foreign Legion. He was a slim yet somewhat swaggering figure, clean-shaven, dark-haired, and blue-eyed, and, as seemed natural in an officer of that famous regiment of victorious failures and successful suicides, he had an air at once dashing and melancholy. He was by birth an Irish gentleman, and in boyhood had known the Galloways—especially Margaret Graham. He had left his country after some crash of debts, and now expressed his complete freedom from British etiquette by swinging about in uniform, sabre and spurs. When he bowed to the Ambassador's family, Lord and Lady Galloway bent stiffly, and Lady Margaret looked away.

But for whatever old causes such people might be interested in each other, their distinguished host was not specially interested in them. No one of them at least was in his eyes the guest of the evening. Valentin was expecting, for special reasons, a man of world-wide fame, whose friendship he had secured during some of his great detective tours and triumphs in the United States. He was expecting Julius K. Brayne, that multi-millionaire whose colossal and even crushing endowments of small religions have occasioned so much easy sport and easier solemnity for the American and English papers. Nobody could quite make out whether Mr. Brayne was an atheist or a Mormon or a Christian Scientist; but he was ready to pour money into any intellectual vessel, so long as it was an untried vessel. One of his hobbies was to wait for the American Shakespeare—a hobby more patient than angling. He admired Walt Whitman, but thought that Luke P. Tanner, of Paris, Pa., was more 'progressive' than Whitman any day. He liked anything that he thought 'progressive.' He thought Valentin 'progressive,' thereby doing him a grave injustice.

The solid appearance of Julius K. Brayne in the room was as decisive as a dinner bell. He had this great quality, which very few of us can claim, that his presence was as big as his absence. He was a huge fellow, as fat as he was tall, clad in complete evening black, without so much relief as a watch-chain or a ring. His hair was white and well brushed back like a German's; his face was red, fierce and cherubic, with one dark tuft under the lower lip that threw up that otherwise infantile visage with an effect theatrical and even Mephistophelean. Not long, however, did that salon merely stare at the celebrated American; his lateness had already become a domestic problem, and he was sent with all speed into the dining-room with Lady Galloway on his arm.

Except on one point the Galloways were genial and casual enough. So long as Lady Margaret did not take the arm of that adventurer O'Brien, her father was quite satisfied; and she had not done so, she had decorously gone in with Dr. Simon. Nevertheless, old Lord Galloway was restless and almost rude. He was diplomatic enough during dinner, but when, over the cigars, three of the younger men—Simon the doctor, Brown the priest, and the detrimental O'Brien, the exile in a foreign uniform—all melted away to mix with the ladies or smoke in the conservatory, then the English diplomatist grew very undiplomatic indeed. He was stung every sixty seconds with the thought that the scamp O'Brien might be signalling to Margaret somehow; he did not attempt to imagine how. He was left over the coffee with Brayne, the hoary Yankee who believed in all religions, and Valentin, the grizzled Frenchman who believed in none. They could argue with each other, but neither could appeal to him. After a time this 'progressive' logomachy had reached a crisis of tedium; Lord Galloway got up also and sought the drawing-room. He lost his way in long passages for some six or eight minutes: till he heard the high-pitched, didactic voice of the doctor, and then the dull voice of the priest, followed by general laughter. They also, he thought with a curse, were probably arguing about 'science and religion.' But the instant he opened the salon door he saw only one thing—he saw what was not there. He saw that Commandant O'Brien was absent, and that Lady Margaret was absent too.

Rising impatiently from the drawing-room, as he had from the dining-room, he stamped along the passage once more. His notion of protecting his daughter from the Irish-Algerian n'er-do-weel had become something central and even mad in his mind. As he went towards the back of the house, where was Valentin's study, he was surprised to meet his daughter, who swept past with a white, scornful face, which was a second enigma. If she had been with O'Brien, where was O'Brien! If she had not been with O'Brien, where had she been? With a sort of senile and passionate suspicion he groped his way to the dark back parts of the mansion, and eventually found a servants' entrance that opened on to the garden. The moon with her scimitar had now ripped up and rolled away all the storm-wrack. The argent light lit up all four corners of the garden. A tall figure in blue was striding across the lawn towards the study door; a glint of moonlit silver on his facings picked him out as Commandant O'Brien.

He vanished through the French windows into the house, leaving Lord Galloway in an indescribable temper, at once virulent and vague. The blue-and-silver garden, like a scene in a theatre, seemed to taunt him with all that tyrannic tenderness against which his worldly authority was at war. The length and grace of the Irishman's stride enraged him as if he were a rival instead of a father; the moonlight maddened him. He was trapped as if by magic into a garden of troubadours, a Watteau fairyland; and, willing to shake off such amorous imbecilities by speech, he stepped briskly after his enemy. As he did so he tripped over some tree or stone in the grass; looked down at it first with irritation and then a second time with curiosity. The next instant the moon and the tall poplars looked at an unusual sight—an elderly English diplomatist running hard and crying or bellowing as he ran.

His hoarse shouts brought a pale face to the study door, the beaming glasses and worried brow of Dr. Simon, who heard the nobleman's first clear words. Lord Galloway was crying: 'A corpse in the grass—a blood-stained corpse.' O'Brien at last had gone utterly out of his mind.

'We must tell Valentin at once,' said the doctor, when the other had brokenly described all that he had dared to examine. 'It is fortunate that he is here'; and even as he spoke the great detective entered the study, attracted by the cry. It was almost amusing to note his typical transformation; he had come with the common concern of a host and a gentleman, fearing that some guest or servant was ill. When he was told the gory fact, he turned with all his gravity instantly bright and businesslike; for this, however abrupt and awful, was his business.

'Strange, gentlemen,' he said as they hurried out into the garden, 'that I should have hunted mysteries all over the earth, and now one comes and settles in my own back-yard. But where is the place?' They crossed the lawn less easily, as a slight mist had begun to rise from the river; but under the guidance of the shaken Galloway they found the body sunken in deep grass—the body of a very tall and broad-shouldered man. He lay face downwards, so they could only see that his big shoulders were clad in black cloth, and that his big head was bald, except for a wisp or two of brown hair that clung to his skull like wet seaweed. A scarlet serpent of blood crawled from under his fallen face.

'At least,' said Simon, with a deep and singular intonation, 'he is none of our party.'

'Examine him, doctor,' cried Valentin rather sharply. 'He may not be dead.'

The doctor bent down. 'He is not quite cold, but I am afraid he is dead enough,' he answered. 'Just help me to lift him up.'

They lifted him carefully an inch from the ground, and all doubts as to his being really dead were settled at once and frightfully. The head fell away. It had been entirely sundered from the body; whoever had cut his throat had managed to sever the neck as well. Even Valentin was slightly shocked. 'He must have been as strong as a gorilla,' he muttered.

Not without a shiver, though he was used to anatomical abortions, Dr. Simon lifted the head. It was slightly slashed about the neck and jaw, but the face was substantially unhurt. It was a ponderous, yellow face, at once sunken and swollen, with a hawk-like nose and heavy lids—a face of a wicked Roman emperor, with, perhaps, a distant touch of a Chinese emperor. All present seemed to look at it with the coldest eye of ignorance. Nothing else could be noted about the man except that, as they had lifted his body, they had seen underneath it the white gleam of a shirt-front defaced with a red gleam of blood. As Dr. Simon said, the man had never been of their party. But he might very well have been trying to join it, for he had come dressed for such an occasion.

Valentin went down on his hands and knees and examined with his closest professional attention the grass and ground for some twenty yards round the body, in which he was assisted less skillfully by the doctor, and quite vaguely by the English lord. Nothing rewarded their grovellings except a few twigs, snapped or chopped into very small lengths, which Valentin lifted for an instant's examination and then tossed away.

'Twigs,' he said gravely; 'twigs, and a total stranger with his head cut off; that is all there is on this lawn.'

There was an almost creepy stillness, and then the unnerved Galloway called out sharply:

'Who's that! Who's that over there by the garden wall!'

A small figure with a foolishly large head drew waveringly near them in the moonlit haze; looked for an instant like a goblin, but turned out to be the harmless little priest whom they had left in the drawing-room.

'I say,' he said meekly, 'there are no gates to this garden, do you know.'

Valentin's black brows had come together somewhat crossly, as they did on principle at the sight of the cassock. But he was far too just a man to deny the relevance of the remark. 'You are right,' he said. 'Before we find out how he came to be killed, we may have to find out how he came to be here. Now listen to me, gentlemen. If it can be done without prejudice to my position and duty, we shall all agree that certain distinguished names might well be kept out of this. There are ladies, gentlemen, and there is a foreign ambassador. If we must mark it down as a crime, then it must be followed up as a crime. But till then I can use my own discretion. I am the head of the police; I am so public that I can afford to be private. Please Heaven, I will clear everyone of my own guests before I call in my men to look for anybody else. Gentlemen, upon your honour, you will none of you leave the house till tomorrow at noon; there are bedrooms for all. Simon, I think you know where to find my man, Ivan, in the front hall; he is a confidential man. Tell him to leave another servant on guard and come to me at once. Lord Galloway, you are certainly the best person to tell the ladies what has happened, and prevent a panic. They also must stay. Father Brown and I will remain with the body.'

When this spirit of the captain spoke in Valentin he was obeyed like a bugle. Dr. Simon went through to the armoury and routed out Ivan, the public detective's private detective.

Galloway went to the drawing-room and told the terrible news tactfully enough, so that by the time the company assembled there the ladies were already startled and already soothed. Meanwhile the good priest and the good atheist stood at the head and foot of the dead man motionless in the moonlight, like symbolic statues of their two philosophies of death.

Ivan, the confidential man with the scar and the moustaches, came out of the house like a cannon-ball, and came racing across the lawn to Valentin like a dog to his master. His livid face was quite lively with the glow of this domestic detective story, and it was with almost unpleasant eagerness that he asked his master's permission to examine the remains.

'Yes; look, if you like, Ivan,' said Valentin, 'but don't be long. We must go in and thrash this out in the house.'

Ivan lifted the head, and then almost let it drop.

'Why,' he gasped, 'it's—no, it isn't; it can't be. Do you know this man, sir?'

'No,' said Valentin indifferently; 'we had better go inside.'

Between them they carried the corpse to a sofa in the study, and then all made their way to the drawing-room.

The detective sat down at a desk quietly, and even without hesitation; but his eye was the iron eye of a judge at assize. He made a few rapid notes upon paper in front of him, and then said shortly: 'Is everybody here?'

'Not Mr. Brayne,' said the Duchess of Mont St. Michel, looking round.

'No,' said Lord Galloway in a hoarse, harsh voice. 'And not Mr. Neil O'Brien, I fancy. I saw that gentleman walking in the garden when the corpse was still warm.'

'Ivan,' said the detective, 'go and fetch Commandant O'Brien and Mr. Brayne. Mr. Brayne, I know, is finishing a cigar in the dining-room; Commandant O'Brien, I think, is walking up and down the conservatory. I am not sure.'

The faithful attendant flashed from the room, and before anyone could stir or speak Valentin went on with the same soldierly swiftness of exposition.

'Everyone here knows that a dead man has been found in the garden, his head cut clean from his body. Dr. Simon, you have examined it. Do you think that to cut a man's throat like that would need great force? Or, perhaps, only a very sharp knife?'

'I should say that it could not be done with a knife at all,' said the pale doctor.

'Have you any thought,' resumed Valentin, 'of a tool with which it could be done?'

'Speaking within modern probabilities, I really haven't,' said the doctor, arching his painful brows. 'It's not easy to hack a neck through even clumsily, and this was a very clean cut. It could be done with a battle-axe or an old headsman's axe, or an old two-handed sword.'

'But, good heavens!' cried the Duchess, almost in hysterics, 'there aren't any two-handed swords and battle-axes round here.'

Valentin was still busy with the paper in front of him. 'Tell me,' he said, still writing rapidly, 'could it have been done with a long French cavalry sabre?'

A low knocking came at the door, which, for some unreasonable reason, curdled everyone's blood like the knocking in Macbeth. Amid that frozen silence Dr. Simon managed to say: 'A sabre—yes, I suppose it could.'

'Thank you,' said Valentin. 'Come in, Ivan.'

The confidential Ivan opened the door and ushered in Commandant Neil O'Brien, whom he had found at last pacing the garden again.

The Irish officer stood up disordered and defiant on the threshold. 'What do you want with me?' he cried.

'Please sit down,' said Valentin in pleasant, level tones.

'Why, you aren't wearing your sword. Where is it?'

'I left it on the library table,' said O'Brien, his brogue deepening in his disturbed mood. 'It was a nuisance, it was getting—'

'Ivan,' said Valentin, 'please go and get the Commandant's sword from the library.' Then, as the servant vanished, 'Lord Galloway says he saw you leaving the garden just before he found the corpse. What were you doing in the garden?'

The Commandant flung himself recklessly into a chair. 'Oh,' he cried in pure Irish, 'admirin' the moon. Communing with Nature, me bhoy.'

A heavy silence sank and endured, and at the end of it came again that trivial and terrible knocking. Ivan reappeared, carrying an empty steel scabbard. 'This is all I can find,' he said.

'Put it on the table,' said Valentin, without looking up.

There was an inhuman silence in the room, like that sea of inhuman silence round the dock of the condemned murderer. The Duchess's weak exclamations had long ago died away. Lord Galloway's swollen hatred was satisfied and even sobered. The voice that came was quite unexpected.

'I think I can tell you,' cried Lady Margaret, in that clear, quivering voice with which a courageous woman speaks publicly. 'I can tell you what Mr. O'Brien was doing in the garden, since he is bound to silence. He was asking me to marry him. I refused; I said in my family circumstances I could give him nothing but my respect. He was a little angry at that; he did not seem to think much of my respect. I wonder,' she added, with rather a wan smile, 'if he will care at all for it now. For I offer it him now. I will swear anywhere that he never did a thing like this.'

Lord Galloway had edged up to his daughter, and was intimidating her in what he imagined to be an undertone. 'Hold your tongue, Maggie,' he said in a thunderous whisper. 'Why should you shield the fellow? Where's his sword? Where's his confounded cavalry—'

He stopped because of the singular stare with which his daughter was regarding him, a look that was indeed a lurid magnet for the whole group.

'You old fool!' she said in a low voice without pretence of piety, 'what do you suppose you are trying to prove? I tell you this man was innocent while with me. But if he wasn't innocent, he was still with me. If he murdered a man in the garden, who was it who must have seen—who must at least have known? Do you hate Neil so much as to put your own daughter—'

Lady Galloway screamed. Everyone else sat tingling at the touch of those satanic tragedies that have been between lovers before now. They saw the proud, white face of the Scotch aristocrat and her lover, the Irish adventurer, like old portraits in a dark house. The long silence was full of formless historical memories of murdered husbands and poisonous paramours.

In the centre of this morbid silence an innocent voice said: 'Was it a very long cigar?'

The change of thought was so sharp that they had to look round to see who had spoken.

'I mean,' said little Father Brown, from the corner of the room, 'I mean that cigar Mr. Brayne is finishing. It seems nearly as long as a walking-stick.'

Despite the irrelevance there was assent as well as irritation in Valentin's face as he lifted his head.

'Quite right,' he remarked sharply. 'Ivan, go and see about Mr. Brayne again, and bring him here at once.'

The instant the factotum had closed the door, Valentin addressed the girl with an entirely new earnestness.

'Lady Margaret,' he said, 'we all feel, I am sure, both gratitude and admiration for your act in rising above your lower dignity and explaining the Commandant's conduct. But there is a hiatus still. Lord Galloway, I understand, met you passing from the study to the drawing-room, and it was only some minutes afterwards that he found the garden and the Commandant still walking there.'

'You have to remember,' replied Margaret, with a faint irony in her voice, 'that I had just refused him, so we should scarcely have come back arm in arm. He is a gentleman, anyhow; and he loitered behind—and so got charged with murder.'

'In those few moments,' said Valentin gravely, 'he might really—'

The knock came again, and Ivan put in his scarred face.

'Beg pardon, sir,' he said, 'but Mr. Brayne has left the house.'

'Left!' cried Valentin, and rose for the first time to his feet.

'Gone. Scooted. Evaporated,' replied Ivan in humorous French. 'His hat and coat are gone, too, and I'll tell you something to cap it all. I ran outside the house to find any traces of him, and I found one, and a big trace, too.'

'What do you mean?' asked Valentin.

'I'll show you,' said his servant, and reappeared with a flashing naked cavalry sabre, streaked with blood about the point and edge. Everyone in the room eyed it as if it were a thunderbolt; but the experienced Ivan went on quite quietly:

'I found this,' he said, 'flung among the bushes fifty yards up the road to Paris. In other words, I found it just where your respectable Mr. Brayne threw it when he ran away.'

There was again a silence, but of a new sort. Valentin took the sabre, examined it, reflected with unaffected concentration of thought, and then turned a respectful face to O'Brien. 'Commandant,' he said, 'we trust you will always produce this weapon if it is wanted for police examination. Meanwhile,' he added, slapping the steel back in the ringing scabbard, 'let me return you your sword.'

At the military symbolism of the action the audience could hardly refrain from applause.

For Neil O'Brien, indeed, that gesture was the turning-point of existence. By the time he was wandering in the mysterious garden again in the colours of the morning the tragic futility of his ordinary mien had fallen from him; he was a man with many reasons for happiness. Lord Galloway was a gentleman, and had offered him an apology. Lady Margaret was something better than a lady, a woman at least, and had perhaps given him something better than an apology, as they drifted among the old flowerbeds before breakfast. The whole company was more lighthearted and humane, for though the riddle of the death remained, the load of suspicion was lifted off them all, and sent flying off to Paris with the strange millionaire—a man they hardly knew. The devil was cast out of the house—he had cast himself out.

Still, the riddle remained; and when O'Brien threw himself on a garden seat beside Dr. Simon, that keenly scientific person at once resumed it. He did not get much talk out of O'Brien, whose thoughts were on pleasanter things.

'I can't say it interests me much,' said the Irishman frankly, 'especially as it seems pretty plain now. Apparently Brayne hated this stranger for some reason; lured him into the garden, and killed him with my sword. Then he fled to the city, tossing the sword away as he went. By the way, Ivan tells me the dead man had a Yankee dollar in his pocket. So he was a countryman of Brayne's, and that seems to clinch it. I don't see any difficulties about the business.'

'There are five colossal difficulties,' said the doctor quietly; 'like high walls within walls. Don't mistake me. I don't doubt that Brayne did it; his flight, I fancy, proves that. But as to how he did it. First difficulty: Why should a man kill another man with a great hulking sabre, when he can almost kill him with a pocket knife and put it back in his pocket? Second difficulty: Why was there no noise or outcry? Does a man commonly see another come up waving a scimitar and offer no remarks? Third difficulty: A servant watched the front door all the evening; and a rat cannot get into Valentin's garden anywhere. How did the dead man get into the garden? Fourth difficulty: Given the same conditions, how did Brayne get out of the garden?'

'And the fifth,' said Neil, with eyes fixed on the English priest who was coming slowly up the path.

'Is a trifle, I suppose,' said the doctor, 'but I think an odd one. When I first saw how the head had been slashed, I supposed the assassin had struck more than once. But on examination I found many cuts across the truncated section; in other words, they were struck after the head was off. Did Brayne hate his foe so fiendishly that he stood sabring his body in the moonlight?'

'Horrible!' said O'Brien, and shuddered.

The little priest, Brown, had arrived while they were talking, and had waited, with characteristic shyness, till they had finished. Then he said awkwardly:

'I say, I'm sorry to interrupt. But I was sent to tell you the news!'

'News?' repeated Simon, and stared at him rather painfully through his glasses.

'Yes, I'm sorry,' said Father Brown mildly. 'There's been another murder, you know.'

Both men on the seat sprang up, leaving it rocking.

'And, what's stranger still,' continued the priest, with his dull eye on the rhododendrons, 'it's the same disgusting sort; it's another beheading. They found the second head actually bleeding into the river, a few yards along Brayne's road to Paris; so they suppose that he—'

'Great Heaven!' cried O'Brien. 'Is Brayne a monomaniac?'

'There are American vendettas,' said the priest impassively.

Then he added: 'They want you to come to the library and see it.'

Commandant O'Brien followed the others towards the inquest, feeling decidedly sick. As a soldier, he loathed all this secretive carnage; where were these extravagant amputations going to stop? First one head was hacked off, and then another; in this case (he told himself bitterly) it was not true that two heads were better than one. As he crossed the study he almost staggered at a shocking coincidence. Upon Valentin's table lay the coloured picture of yet a third bleeding head; and it was the head of Valentin himself. A second glance showed him it was only a Nationalist paper, called The Guillotine, which every week showed one of its political opponents with rolling eyes and writhing features just after execution; for Valentin was an anti-clerical of some note. But O'Brien was an Irishman, with a kind of chastity even in his sins; and his gorge rose against that great brutality of the intellect which belongs only to France. He felt Paris as a whole, from the grotesques on the Gothic churches to the gross caricatures in the newspapers. He remembered the gigantic jests of the Revolution. He saw the whole city as one ugly energy, from the sanguinary sketch lying on Valentin's table up to where, above a mountain and forest of gargoyles, the great devil grins on Notre Dame.

The library was long, low, and dark; what light entered it shot from under low blinds and had still some of the ruddy tinge of morning. Valentin and his servant Ivan were waiting for them at the upper end of a long, slightly-sloping desk, on which lay the mortal remains, looking enormous in the twilight. The big black figure and yellow face of the man found in the garden confronted them essentially unchanged. The second head, which had been fished from among the river reeds that morning, lay streaming and dripping beside it; Valentin's men were still seeking to recover the rest of this second corpse, which was supposed to be afloat. Father Brown, who did not seem to share O'Brien's sensibilities in the least, went up to the second head and examined it with his blinking care. It was little more than a mop of wet white hair, fringed with silver fire in the red and level morning light; the face, which seemed of an ugly, empurpled and perhaps criminal type, had been much battered against trees or stones as it tossed in the water.

'Good morning, Commandant O'Brien,' said Valentin, with quiet cordiality. 'You have heard of Brayne's last experiment in butchery, I suppose?'

Father Brown was still bending over the head with white hair, and he said, without looking up:

'I suppose it is quite certain that Brayne cut off this head, too.'

'Well, it seems common sense,' said Valentin, with his hands in his pockets. 'Killed in the same way as the other. Found within a few yards of the other. And sliced by the same weapon which we know he carried away.'

'Yes, yes; I know,' replied Father Brown submissively. 'Yet, you know, I doubt whether Brayne could have cut off this head.'

'Why not?' inquired Dr. Simon, with a rational stare.

'Well, doctor,' said the priest, looking up blinking, 'can a man cut off his own head? I don't know.'

O'Brien felt an insane universe crashing about his ears; but the doctor sprang forward with impetuous practicality and pushed back the wet white hair.

'Oh, there's no doubt it's Brayne,' said the priest quietly. 'He had exactly that chip in the left ear.'

The detective, who had been regarding the priest with steady and glittering eyes, opened his clenched mouth and said sharply: 'You seem to know a lot about him, Father Brown.'

'I do,' said the little man simply. 'I've been about with him for some weeks. He was thinking of joining our church.'

The star of the fanatic sprang into Valentin's eyes; he strode towards the priest with clenched hands. 'And, perhaps,' he cried, with a blasting sneer, 'perhaps he was also thinking of leaving all his money to your church.'

'Perhaps he was,' said Brown stolidly; 'it is possible.'

'In that case,' cried Valentin, with a dreadful smile, 'you may indeed know a great deal about him. About his life and about his—'

Commandant O'Brien laid a hand on Valentin's arm. 'Drop that slanderous rubbish, Valentin,' he said, 'or there may be more swords yet.'

But Valentin (under the steady, humble gaze of the priest) had already recovered himself. 'Well,' he said shortly, 'people's private opinions can wait. You gentlemen are still bound by your promise to stay; you must enforce it on yourselves—and on each other. Ivan here will tell you anything more you want to know; I must get to business and write to the authorities. We can't keep this quiet any longer. I shall be writing in my study if there is any more news.'

'Is there any more news, Ivan?' asked Dr. Simon, as the chief of police strode out of the room.

'Only one more thing, I think, sir,' said Ivan, wrinkling up his grey old face, 'but that's important, too, in its way. There's that old buffer you found on the lawn,' and he pointed without pretence of reverence at the big black body with the yellow head. 'We've found out who he is, anyhow.'

'Indeed!' cried the astonished doctor, 'and who is he?'

'His name was Arnold Becker,' said the under-detective, 'though he went by many aliases. He was a wandering sort of scamp, and is known to have been in America; so that was where Brayne got his knife into him. We didn't have much to do with him ourselves, for he worked mostly in Germany. We've communicated, of course, with the German police. But, oddly enough, there was a twin brother of his, named Louis Becker, whom we had a great deal to do with. In fact, we found it necessary to guillotine him only yesterday. Well, it's a rum thing, gentlemen, but when I saw that fellow flat on the lawn I had the greatest jump of my life. If I hadn't seen Louis Becker guillotined with my own eyes, I'd have sworn it was Louis Becker lying there in the grass. Then, of course, I remembered his twin brother in Germany, and following up the clue—'

The explanatory Ivan stopped, for the excellent reason that nobody was listening to him. The Commandant and the doctor were both staring at Father Brown, who had sprung stiffly to his feet, and was holding his temples tight like a man in sudden and violent pain.

'Stop, stop, stop!' he cried; 'stop talking a minute, for I see half. Will God give me strength? Will my brain make the one jump and see all? Heaven help me! I used to be fairly good at thinking. I could paraphrase any page in Aquinas once. Will my head split—or will it see? I see half—I only see half.'

He buried his head in his hands, and stood in a sort of rigid torture of thought or prayer, while the other three could only go on staring at this last prodigy of their wild twelve hours.

When Father Brown's hands fell they showed a face quite fresh and serious, like a child's. He heaved a huge sigh, and said: 'Let us get this said and done with as quickly as possible. Look here, this will be the quickest way to convince you all of the truth.' He turned to the doctor. 'Dr. Simon,' he said, 'you have a strong head-piece, and I heard you this morning asking the five hardest questions about this business. Well, if you will ask them again, I will answer them.'

Simon's pince-nez dropped from his nose in his doubt and wonder, but he answered at once. 'Well, the first question, you know, is why a man should kill another with a clumsy sabre at all when a man can kill with a bodkin?'

'A man cannot behead with a bodkin,' said Brown calmly, 'and for this murder beheading was absolutely necessary.'

'Why?' asked O'Brien, with interest.

'And the next question?' asked Father Brown.

'Well, why didn't the man cry out or anything?' asked the doctor; 'sabres in gardens are certainly unusual.'

'Twigs,' said the priest gloomily, and turned to the window which looked on the scene of death. 'No one saw the point of the twigs. Why should they lie on that lawn (look at it) so far from any tree? They were not snapped off; they were chopped off. The murderer occupied his enemy with some tricks with the sabre, showing how he could cut a branch in mid-air, or what-not. Then, while his enemy bent down to see the result, a silent slash, and the head fell.'

'Well,' said the doctor slowly, 'that seems plausible enough. But my next two questions will stump anyone.'

The priest still stood looking critically out of the window and waited.

'You know how all the garden was sealed up like an air-tight chamber,' went on the doctor. 'Well, how did the strange man get into the garden?'

Without turning round, the little priest answered: 'There never was any strange man in the garden.'

There was a silence, and then a sudden cackle of almost childish laughter relieved the strain. The absurdity of Brown's remark moved Ivan to open taunts.

'Oh!' he cried; 'then we didn't lug a great fat corpse on to a sofa last night? He hadn't got into the garden, I suppose?'

'Got into the garden?' repeated Brown reflectively. 'No, not entirely.'

'Hang it all,' cried Simon, 'a man gets into a garden, or he doesn't.'

'Not necessarily,' said the priest, with a faint smile. 'What is the next question, doctor?'

'I fancy you're ill,' exclaimed Dr. Simon sharply; 'but I'll ask the next question if you like. How did Brayne get out of the garden?'

'He didn't get out of the garden,' said the priest, still looking out of the window.

'Didn't get out of the garden?' exploded Simon.

'Not completely,' said Father Brown.

Simon shook his fists in a frenzy of French logic. 'A man gets out of a garden, or he doesn't,' he cried.

'Not always,' said Father Brown.

Dr. Simon sprang to his feet impatiently. 'I have no time to spare on such senseless talk,' he cried angrily. 'If you can't understand a man being on one side of a wall or the other, I won't trouble you further.'

'Doctor,' said the cleric very gently, 'we have always got on very pleasantly together. If only for the sake of old friendship, stop and tell me your fifth question.'

The impatient Simon sank into a chair by the door and said briefly: 'The head and shoulders were cut about in a queer way. It seemed to be done after death.'

'Yes,' said the motionless priest, 'it was done so as to make you assume exactly the one simple falsehood that you did assume. It was done to make you take for granted that the head belonged to the body.'

The borderland of the brain, where all the monsters are made, moved horribly in the Gaelic O'Brien. He felt the chaotic presence of all the horse-men and fish-women that man's unnatural fancy has begotten. A voice older than his first fathers seemed saying in his ear: 'Keep out of the monstrous garden where grows the tree with double fruit. Avoid the evil garden where died the man with two heads.' Yet, while these shameful symbolic shapes passed across the ancient mirror of his Irish soul, his Frenchified intellect was quite alert, and was watching the odd priest as closely and incredulously as all the rest.

Father Brown had turned round at last, and stood against the window, with his face in dense shadow; but even in that shadow they could see it was pale as ashes. Nevertheless, he spoke quite sensibly, as if there were no Gaelic souls on earth.

'Gentlemen,' he said, 'you did not find the strange body of Becker in the garden. You did not find any strange body in the garden. In face of Dr. Simon's rationalism, I still affirm that Becker was only partly present. Look here!' (pointing to the black bulk of the mysterious corpse) 'you never saw that man in your lives. Did you ever see this man?'

He rapidly rolled away the bald, yellow head of the unknown, and put in its place the white-maned head beside it. And there, complete, unified, unmistakable, lay Julius K. Brayne.

'The murderer,' went on Brown quietly, 'hacked off his enemy's head and flung the sword far over the wall. But he was too clever to fling the sword only. He flung the head over the wall also. Then he had only to clap on another head to the corpse, and (as he insisted on a private inquest) you all imagined a totally new man.'

'Clap on another head!' said O'Brien staring. 'What other head? Heads don't grow on garden bushes, do they?'

'No,' said Father Brown huskily, and looking at his boots; 'there is only one place where they grow. They grow in the basket of the guillotine, beside which the chief of police, Aristide Valentin, was standing not an hour before the murder. Oh, my friends, hear me a minute more before you tear me in pieces. Valentin is an honest man, if being mad for an arguable cause is honesty. But did you never see in that cold, grey eye of his that he is mad! He would do anything, anything, to break what he calls the superstition of the Cross. He has fought for it and starved for it, and now he has murdered for it. Brayne's crazy millions had hitherto been scattered among so many sects that they did little to alter the balance of things. But Valentin heard a whisper that Brayne, like so many scatter-brained sceptics, was drifting to us; and that was quite a different thing. Brayne would pour supplies into the impoverished and pugnacious Church of France; he would support six Nationalist newspapers like The Guillotine. The battle was already balanced on a point, and the fanatic took flame at the risk. He resolved to destroy the millionaire, and he did it as one would expect the greatest of detectives to commit his only crime. He abstracted the severed head of Becker on some criminological excuse, and took it home in his official box. He had that last argument with Brayne, that Lord Galloway did not hear the end of; that failing, he led him out into the sealed garden, talked about swordsmanship, used twigs and a sabre for illustration, and—'

Ivan of the Scar sprang up. 'You lunatic,' he yelled; 'you'll go to my master now, if I take you by—'

'Why, I was going there,' said Brown heavily; 'I must ask him to confess, and all that.'

Driving the unhappy Brown before them like a hostage or sacrifice, they rushed together into the sudden stillness of Valentin's study.

The great detective sat at his desk apparently too occupied to hear their turbulent entrance. They paused a moment, and then something in the look of that upright and elegant back made the doctor run forward suddenly. A touch and a glance showed him that there was a small box of pills at Valentin's elbow, and that Valentin was dead in his chair; and on the blind face of the suicide was more than the pride of Cato.

ABOUT TERRY O'BRIEN

Terry O'Brien is an academic with three decades of experience in teaching language and communication skills in India and abroad. He also headed a college under the auspices of the University of Delhi.

A prolific writer, with several books to his credit, Terry O'Brien is a reputed professional motivational speaker and a quizmaster.